Grottogate

Also by Peter K. Connolly:

The Last Slider

When Shadows Fell at Notre Dame

Grottogate

Peter K. Connolly

iUniverse, Inc.
New York Bloomington

Grottogate

iUniverse books may be ordered through booksellers or by contacting:

iUniverse
1663 Liberty Drive
Bloomington, IN 47403
www.iuniverse.com
1-800-Authors (1-800-288-4677)

ISBN: 978-1-4502-6422-8 (sc)
ISBN: 978-1-4502-6423-5 (dj)
ISBN: 978-1-4502-6424-2 (ebk)

Library of Congress Control Number: 2010915045

Printed in the United States of America

iUniverse rev. date: 10/7/2010

To Richard Savage, loyal friend, Notre Dame's #1 centenarian and family patriarch who has lived a life of true Catholicity and goodness, and whose dedication to his alma mater and to the Blessed Virgin Mary is inimitable.

Epigraph

Watergate (wôtr-gāt′): A scandal in Washington, DC, involving abuse of power … and obstruction of justice.

Grottogate (Grot'to-gāt′): A scandal in Notre Dame, IN, involving abuse of power … and obstruction of justice.

Acknowledgments

This book was inspired in part by (and I thank them) ND Response and all those students, clerics, alumni, and friends who stood tall before Mary Immaculate at the Notre Dame Grotto on May 17, 2009 and prayed the Rosary in reparation for the university honoring the high king of abortion.

For my days at Stonehill College, I am ever grateful to Reverend Francis Edward Grogan, CSC, a kind and gentle man, graduate of Notre Dame and good friend to so many. Father Grogan lost his life as a passenger aboard United Airlines Flight 175 on 9/11/01.

No one inspired me more than the late Dr. Ralph McInerney, both bedrock and tower of strength of the Church. The personification of intellectual excellence, he was professor of philosophy and medieval studies at Notre Dame, prolific author, scholar, and unblinking, passionate critic of ND's eroding Catholic core during his fifty-five years on campus.

The Lord blessed me the day he sent me to Mary Daly Joyce of Missouri, a God-fearing, faithful friend and daughter of Eugene Daly, the "piper" aboard the *Titanic* who survived to return to Ireland. I treasure Mary's memories and moral support.

I can never give enough thanks to my dearest sister Kate Connolly, peerless poet and writer, and shining beacon of healing light to me and to so many others. Her contributions to this book and to strengthening my resolve were limitless.

Finally, my most loving Joann Aldridge has been an enduring wellspring of optimism and has kept me happy and healthy for many years. She edited my manuscripts and cheerfully endured evenings of profound silence as I fumbled and stumbled through plots and subplots.

PROLOGUE

Shelby and I still make it a point to first visit Our Lady of Lourdes Grotto when we return to North America and to the University of Notre Dame campus. Gerry Finn did the same. Coach Gerry Faust did also. Leo Darcy with Act For Aquinas did as well. And I'm sure there were many others.

The Grotto. It's been there since 1896, 146 years ago, flickering fingers of fire beckoning to a nearby ancient sycamore that has its own stories to tell. A glade of serenity whose tranquility not even repeated acts of arson and destruction can unsettle. It's obvious that the charred granite, gate railing, and rocks have not been cleaned in some time. Nor has the statue of Our Lady, wellspring of consolation and grantor of gifts.

The two relics brought long ago from Lourdes, France—and cemented in stone—are no longer visible. A metal horseshoe barrier has been erected to prevent visitors from getting too close. It matters not, since now there are only two candles, both electric, unreachable beyond the gates. Their yellow glow is barely perceptible in the November dusk. A plaque from the class of 1955 has been rendered unreadable by a chisel, it would appear. A nearby lean-to shelters a stack of prayer rugs. A stained, slotted metal box hangs from a tree with a sign: "Make a donation and Make a wish."

Make a wish? A wish? We kneel on the sidewalk and offer a prayer. A prayer to Our Lady that it is not yet too late for Notre Dame, for America, to turn it all around. It is the two hundredth anniversary of the founding of Notre Dame and we look forward to meeting with our old friend Father Frank Fischer, now the university's eighteenth president and successor to the late Father Henry Ignatius Pankey. His will be a Sisyphean task.

We remember those days when we sat side by side in Notre Dame's Sports Information department, hoping for yet another season of glory for the Fighting Irish. And we remember thirty years back when Gerry Finn was alive. And the excitement and sadness of it all.

Josh Allen, Nov. 3, 2042

Chapter 1

Katherine Curran Finn
Queenstown, Ireland
April 11, 1912

"Receive into thy most gracious protection the persons of us, thy servants, and the ship in which we sail. Preserve us from the dangers of the sea."

Kate Curran Finn whispered her quick prayer to St. Brendan yet again as she and her sister Nora joined the crush of men, women, and children shuffling along Queenstown's timeworn Deepwater Quay. The southwest wind was tossing the incoming tide against the stacked-stone wall, spawning an occasional icy-cold spray over them. The bright red and white, twin-tailed pennant of the British White Star Line snapped in the early April gusts and festive signal flags of all colors flapped noisily on lines strung over the wharf.

A leathered old man, down on one knee, slid a slippery, shiny mackerel into a well-worn, battered bucket. He reached toward their legs with four groping, discolored fingers and gave them a rubbery, toothless smile as they hastened by him.

Kate moved aside, clutching a red carpetbag with one hand and pressing down on her flowered broad-brim hat with the other. Nora held Kate's arm, her mood as dark as the black water slapping the quay wall. She silently scolded Kate's husband of three months, Michael Finn, who was absent today.

Michael Finn of the *Sinn Féin*. A *Shinner*. And, true to his own name, a proud member of the Fenian Brotherhood with just that one driving obsession: free Ireland of British rule.

Nora shivered. *Why am I feeling so fearful? This can't be wise. My dear, trusting sister Kate, to be crossing the Atlantic—with child. And Michael should be here with his wife. Please, Mary, Star of the Sea, safeguard all seafarers.*

Nora shook her head as she glanced at Kate, setting off with her little bag and Michael's money in her pocket.

"You'll be writing me now, Nora," said Kate. "Let me know when Michael will be coming, promise? I think he'll not be much for letters. I pray he'll be there for the birth of our little one."

"Of course I'll write, you silly goose. We'll both be there when the time comes. Maybe even sell the farm and be gone with County Cavan! You've your ticket?" she asked for the third time.

"Aye, and the thirty pounds from Michael."

Thirty pounds, thought Nora. *Thirty. Ah, yes. Gospel of John.* But she said nothing and pulled her younger sister closer to her. "Tell Nell and Uncle Will I love them. Soon we'll all be together again."

America, one of two side-wheel, single-stack transfer tenders owned by Clyde Shipping, had checked in most of the 113 third-class men, women, and children bound for New York. Once they were ferried to—and boarded—the 880-foot goliath now riding at anchor near Roche's Point, none would complain that there was only one bath for all of the men—and one bath for all of the women and children. Two baths for 706 persons on the lower decks. Perfectly fine. It was common knowledge that frequent baths caused lung disease.

Steerage class, yes, but far more comfortable accommodations than most Irish enjoyed in their own homes.

"It's time, Katie."

Nora could no longer hold back the flood of tears that had been rising since they left home. She hurled her arms around her younger sister and sobbed on one frail shoulder. She could feel the chill of Kate's body under the thin cloth.

Kate stroked her sister's hair. "Not a worry now, Nora. Not a worry."

Nora just shuddered. *Ah, and it's I who should be doing the comforting!*

A single bell in the spired tower of St. Colman's Cathedral on the nearby hillside had begun tolling at noon. It would not stop until the massive black-hulled, four-funnel ship departed on its maiden voyage at 1:30 that afternoon.

Other passengers had boarded a second tender, *Ireland*, as had the "Gentlemen of the Press" hoping for a brief visit to the triple-screw steamer. On the quay, a handful of shrouded photographers remained, steadying their cameras, none with any premonition of the peril of the passage.

No room for words, but there were none satisfactory. Teary-eyed, the sisters embraced again.

Kate stepped on the gangway of *America* and smiled at the young man assisting her. "Mind your steps going up, ma'am. Watch those boards."

She turned and made her way up the wobbly planks. Another man with muttonchop sideburns reached out and helped her. She quickly joined others along a rail on the crowded upper deck. It was only minutes before crewmen began to cast off. She felt a chill and clung to her bag. Would she ever see Nora again?

The wind picked up as the boat slowly moved away. Billowing loaves of dark gray clouds drifted overhead. Her doubts retreated at the thoughts of seeing America, her sister Nell, her Uncle Will and, most of all, of having her child there with, hopefully, husband Michael at her side.

She'd lost sight of Nora but continued to wave in the direction of the wharf and look back with some uneasiness as the coast of Ireland and the brightly colored homes in Queenstown diminished in the distance.

They passed from the harbor into open water, and the tender made its way toward Roche's Point lighthouse. All stood fascinated as the ten-story ship that would take them to America came into view in Ringabella Bay. They shook their heads in wonder. "Unthinkable," Kate thought she heard someone say. But she couldn't take her eyes off the ship. *It is indeed titanic.*

The tender drew alongside Royal Mail Ship *Titanic* and the gangway came down. Kate felt herself jostled as the crowd queued up. Some were pointing up with alarm at one of the ship's four huge funnels. Kate followed their eyes and was unnerved to see a black-faced figure clinging to the top of the funnel. *This should not be.* When she looked again, it was gone.

The line began to move more quickly, and Kate soon found herself stepping onto the lower deck. She surrendered her ticket to a white-capped young man in a red, four-buttoned jacket. He scanned his clipboard and nodded.

"Ah, yes, Kate Curran. Ticket number 370373. County Cavan." He scanned his list and smiled. "Did you know there's another Kate Curran sailing with us? Tipperary. A bit older. Not quite as lovely. But don't you be telling her now what I said. You'll meet her, I'm sure."

"I'll try to find her," said Kate. "I don't know anyone else I'll be traveling with. Thank you."

The young man blushed and smiled again. "You do love your Kates! No offense, Miss Curran. I've a cousin in County Cavan. Do you know the name O'Donnell there?"

Now it was Kate's turn to smile. "Ahh, they're as thick as primrose, are they not?"

He pointed to anther queue. "You'll have to join them over there now, Miss Curran. Eye examinations."

She hesitated a moment. "Sir? My married name is Finn. I was a Curran when I paid the seven pounds fifteen for my ticket."

He laughed. "That's fine, Mrs. Finn. You'll get used to it, I'm sure."

Later that afternoon, as hundreds of screaming Herring Gulls trailed in its frothy white wake, the ship passed below the headlands of Kinsale and sounded her whistle for a gaggle of gaping onlookers before heading into the open sea.

On the third-class promenade "C" Deck, a group was singing *Erin's Lament* to the accompaniment of a *Uilleann* piper, a rail-thin young man whose name, Kate later learned, was Edward Dolan. Like her Michael—and many other young Irishmen—Dolan strongly opposed

British rule and didn't try to hide it. "*To Erin's sons be gracious, who in sorrow are forced from their homes …*"

His lyrics told it all. "*They set the roof on fire with their cursed English spleen. And that's another reason why I left old Skibbereen …*"

Dolan had decided to travel abroad and test the waters. He was an ardent nationalist, a *Shinner* like Kate's husband, Michael. He believed that there were many Americans who would lend their support to the cause. His talents with the elbow pipes had opened doors and he displayed them now for his steerage-class audience.

"*Oh, I courted girls in Blarney … in Queenstown … Cove of Cork … and the next that you will hear of me … is a letter from New York.*"

Chapter 2

370 miles south of Newfoundland
2:30 am, April 15, 1912

In the end, it was the gaunt young music-maker, Edward Dolan from her neighboring County Westmeath, to whom Kate Curran Finn would owe her life. And the life of her child. Less than twelve hours earlier, Dolan had been once again squeezing out jigs and reels on the steerage deck and Kate herself had been step-dancing to the ancient tunes.

Now, on that starry but moonless Sunday night when more than fifteen hundred souls would perish in the hypothermic North Atlantic (many within just minutes of being immersed), the piper became Kate's lifeline. As she clung to a brass button on his overcoat, Dolan pulled her from the frigid, floe-filled waters and wrapped his large, black woolen coat around them both, the heat of their bodies keeping them alive in a "collapsible" lifeboat until they were transferred to Lifeboat 14 and then rescued by Cunard Line's RMS *Carpathia* crewmen just after dawn.

They were given warm clothing, blankets, soup, and hot drinks, and then taken to first aid rooms that had been set up in the ship's three dining rooms. Others requiring more assistance were moved to cots in a recovery room where *Carpathia* passengers joined in caring for them.

Less than six hours after the rescue, the ship's under-officers conducted a roll call in the saloon, collecting names and other information to assemble a manifest of *Titanic*'s saloon, cabin, and steerage survivors.

Two days later, as *Carpathia* neared New York, the completed list was checked with the survivors.

Kate remembered in time and turned to the young officer with two gold stripes on the sleeve of his blue uniform. "It should be Finn, sir. I was a Curran only three months ago. Kate Curran. But now I'm Kate Finn. And soon to be a mam."

The young man drew a dark line through "Curran" and inserted "Finn." Then added "w/child." He showed her the list. "There. Kate Curran, now Kate Finn. Of County Cavan. Welcome to America, Mrs. Finn! The Lord looked after you. You and your babe!"

The White Star Line homeport of the International Navigation Company had become a funeral parlor. At New York's Chelsea Piers in a chilling rain, a somber, swelling assemblage of thousands crowded Cunard Line's Pier 54 as *Carpathia* was nosed alongside just before 10 PM to offload four shrouded bodies and 705 *Titanic* survivors, less than a third of the 2,223 passengers and crew who had sailed on her maiden voyage.

It was more than an hour before Kate finally reached the metal gangway. She wore her dried clothes, a donated seaman's jacket, and carried a blue cloth bag containing a new mouthbrush, comb, hairbrush, towel, some personal effects, and the brass button that she had torn from the overcoat of her rescuer, the piper Edward Dolan. She was stopped at the bottom by a red-eyed, lanky, tired-looking official in a wet, woolen uniform.

"Your name, Miss?"

"Please, please, let me off. It's Kate Finn." She felt dizzy. The man shouted her name into a bullhorn as he stepped aside. For Kate, who had been on the *Titanic* for almost four days, immersed for several hours in the numbing North Atlantic, spent a night in a crowded lifeboat, and then another four bewildering days aboard the *Carpathia*, it was a nightmare.

But the worst lay ahead for Kate. In the ensuing clamor, confusion, and crush of humanity, she was met not by her sister Nell but by a young woman in a nurse's uniform who stepped forward quickly, a Sister of Charity nurse, one of many who were taking some one hundred survivors, most now widows and orphans, to St. Vincent Hospital for the night. Amidst scenes of rejoicing and scenes of grief, the nurse guided Kate to the end of the pier and sat her down out of the rain.

"I'm Sister Margaret Timothy, Kate."

"Where …?"

She put her hands on Kate's shoulders to steady her.

"Nell, your sister Nell, was to meet you, Kate?"

"Yes, yes, where is she?"

"Do you have any other relatives here?"

"No … Yes, my Uncle Will Curran in Newark. Where is …?"

"I'm so sorry. So sorry, Kate." The nurse reached out and pulled Kate close. "Your sister's heart gave out when she saw your name on the list of those missing. I don't know why it was there. Just a mistake. So much confusion. So many gone. I'm very, very sorry. We'll take care …"

Kate collapsed into her arms.

The days that immediately followed were lost to Kate's memory forever. She and others were interviewed by inspectors with the Immigration Service. She scarcely recognized her Uncle Will when he arrived two days later at the hospital to take her to his home. Her sister Nell's funeral had been that morning at Nell's parish church, St. Ignatius Loyola on East Eighty-fourth Street. Uncle Will, City Attorney of Newark, had many friends in Manhattan and he had coordinated all details, as well as disposition of Nell's ground floor apartment in the seven-story brownstone building at 309 East Eighty-eighth Street.

He thanked the Sisters of Charity and pressed two Grover Cleveland twenty-dollar notes into Sister Margaret's hand. Then he helped Kate into his Steamer Roadster and fired up the boiler.

"They told Nell you didn't make it. They said there was no doubt. Showed her a list of those lost. You were on it. I saw it myself. Kate Curran. A black-edged list marked 'Final.'"

"But there was another Kate Curran … I never met …"

"It will be all right. And may the Lord bless that good Sister Margaret. And all of them at St. Vincent."

But what of my baby?

Will went on. "I'm really sorry that I wasn't at the pier to meet you. I was in Philadelphia when the messenger from the hospital arrived at home."

Kate just stared. "What pier?" she asked.

"End of the line," he said an hour later. He sounded the brass bulb horn and pulled up in front of a three-story, brownstone brick, turreted row house at 241 South Eighth Street in Newark. Nine stone steps and a black iron railing led up to a mahogany door with decorative inlaid frosted glass.

"I own this block. We have our masquerades in the adjoining house on the right there. Now you'll finally get to meet your cousins."

Clouds of steam poured from pipes below the headlights and another at the rear. Kate looked out to see several small faces smiling down from the tall, narrow windows.

"I'm tired, Uncle Will. My baby is tired too. I need to tell Nora about Nell."

"I've done that, Kate. Sent a cable to Michael and Nora. And everything will be okay. Sister Margaret said your babe has a good strong heartbeat.

"Not to worry. You can rest here for a few days. I'll settle you out in the country. I've a comforting summer home in Somerset County. Apple trees, a brook of fat fish, pheasants, wild strawberries as big as your fist, plums, grapes, and horses. There's a housekeeper. You can just sit in the sun. You'll love it. And your little one can be born at All Souls Hospital. It's close by, and Bishop O'Connor and Sister Superior Viola, who oversee it, are both good friends of mine. I'm very sorry for the loss of Nell, Kate."

"I need to write to Michael."

It was the summer of 1912. New Yorkers were still agonizing over the loss of friends and relatives on the Titanic—less than a year, they deplored, after the horrific deaths by fire of more than 140 young Jewish and Italian workers at the Triangle Shirtwaist garment factory at the foot of Fifth Avenue.

Arizona had just become the forty-eighth state and the forgotten Inca city of Machu Picchu had been recently "rediscovered." Jim Thorpe had won two golds at the Olympics in Stockholm, and Uncle Will was busy campaigning for his good friend New Jersey Governor Woodrow Wilson.

But Kate, *prima gravida*, swimming deep into her first and only pregnancy, cared nothing of any of it as she lay on a hillside overlooking Clairvaux Manor, Uncle Will's country home in Somerset County.

A letter from Nora rested on the warm, rich, black New Jersey earth beside her, unread except for the first few sentences. She could scarcely breathe. First her widowed sister Nell, dying just hours before they'd been reunited. And now, her husband Michael, struck down by the kick of a horse. *My poor little fatherless babe.*

Chapter 3

Josh Allen
Notre Dame, IN
November 2011

I was not happy back in 1998 when my father announced that he was being transferred to Indianapolis. And I was expected to move with my parents from Massachusetts to the Hoosier state. My older brother Alan, who'd recently married, would remain. I'd just finished my second year at Stonehill College in North Easton, less than an hour's drive from our bayside home on George's Rock Road in Sandwich, Cape Cod's oldest town.

Stonehill, run by the Holy Cross Congregation, the same order that founded Notre Dame, would be tough to leave. I was one of the few students living off campus and life was good. Very good. But that's another story.

I'd loved Stonehill's historic and shaggy oasis of a campus and I'd done well there. Good marks and I'd been a linebacker on the varsity football team. I'd made a lot of friends, students and faculty, and we were a plank member of the highly regarded Northeast-10 Conference. So I rebelled, but not too loudly.

"Why can't I just stay and finish my last two years here? I could live with Alan."

My father smiled. "Josh, believe me, I know just how you feel. I've been losing sleep over it. But I think you'll like the solution. I've talked to your registrar, Father McPherson, and he assured me that he can arrange for your transfer to Notre Dame. With no loss of credits. Besides, Alan and Barbara have their own lives to lead and three's a crowd in a one-bedroom apartment."

He shook his head. "I'm sorry. I don't have a choice about my job. And no need to tell you that your college football days are probably over. But when you leave ND in two years with that degree in your back pocket, you'll be a happy guy. And you'll have a lot of doors opened to you. You'll need those open doors to help you pay off student loans."

I tried to be a walk-on at ND but came to my senses quickly. I was a flea in a nest of killer bees. Now, some thirteen years later, I'd paid off my loans and I was a proud member of ND's first graduating class of the new millenium. Along the way, I'd lost my father to cancer and my mother to an enterprising, but boring, VP at Naptown's Eli Lilly headquarters.

I'd also lost whatever respect I might once have had for Mubaraq El Baba, the narcissistic "Progressive" dictator in the White House who'd suddenly intruded into our lives, divided friends and families, and publicly derided America before its enemies. His National Civilian Security Force (NCSF), made up of mostly high school dropouts and former welfare recipients, had bullied our country into a federal police state. Piece by piece, this messiah-turned-pariah had dismantled the foundations of America and ravaged the Treasury and the souls of its citizens. Sam Adams and George Washington would have wept with anger. And retaliated.

But now this was a nation in handcuffs. Citizen uprisings were snuffed out like picnic bonfires. Gun ownership was outlawed and the Internet was under tight surveillance as the result of the "kill switch" that allowed the government to shut it down in the case of a national emergency. And those became as frequent as the tornado warning tests that were once a monthly first Monday occurrence.

On the plus side, I was grateful for my media relations (football) job in ND's Sports Info department. I'd moved up quickly. Before that, my only work experience was two years in a small PR firm in Indianapolis.

And I was in love, head over heels, with an office colleague, the delightful-delovely, ravishing redhead Shelby Lester of the cat's eyes. She was twenty-seven, five years my junior, and a Saint Mary's College grad by way of Virginia's Tidewater. With only one failing. She was a bird watcher who would have interrupted an audience with the Pope and his red-caped Cardinals to eyeball a Purple-naped Lory on the windowsill. As far as I could tell, the sight of a rare bird was the only thing that could render her speechless.

But I still savored memories of those four intoxicating semesters I'd spent in the late '90s at Stonehill and—especially during these dwindling autumn days—the indefinable, misty enchantment and salty scent of New England. There were other private memories, but I'd put them behind me.

And now. Now I could hardly contain myself with the news—as yet unannounced—that the Notre Dame and Stonehill gridders would be going head-to-head next November. In my lifetime I'd never have thought it possible.

I'd been tipped off earlier this week in an e-mail from my old friend Ed Wagner, Stonehill's communications vice president. I tried to imagine how it might be recorded, fifty years from now, by a scribe in the annals of NCAA football—by someone who also quietly dared to question our country's suffocating socialistic path:

> *It was a long time coming. Sixty years (two generations) passed before the first football game between New England upstart Stonehill College, founded in 1948, and its big, big brother, the University of Notre Dame, for a century the most respected—if not always revered—name in the sport.*
>
> *Stonehill vs. Notre Dame. Both, ostensibly, institutions of the Holy Cross Congregation (Congregatio a Sancta Cruce). Both, ostensibly, Catholic institutions of higher learning.*
>
> *But institutions have a way of changing.*
> *As do governments.*
> *And, as does history.*

Then I thought of how my father would have seen this unlikely match-up. *Surely these are two schools light years apart in terms of athletic excellence*, he'd have said. *How could this happen?*

He'd died less than a year after I graduated. I thanked God he was able to see me capped and gowned as our class of 2000, traditionally, walked down the steps of ND's Main Building.

What was it that brought the once invincible Fighting Irish to this? Now, at age thirty-two, I thought I understood. For starters, the new century had been unkind—and even punishing—to the team. But that was both on and off the football field. Bone-headed play-calling and needless penalties. Grandstanding, taunting, and inflated egos. Lackluster recruiting. Player focus not on teamwork but on finding a launch pad into the National Felon League. Together, they precipitated an alarming and untenable number of losses, followed quickly by undisguised alumni exasperation. I was a fledgling alumnus then, and too naïve to understand it all. I made no connection between the fortunes of the football team and the politics of the administration.

In hindsight, it was much more than football. Very much more. For more than forty years the ND administration had been making a covert left turn away from the deeply rooted Catholic principles on which the university was founded. In the late 1960s, control was quietly transferred from the Holy Cross Congregation to a twelve-person (half non-clerical) Board of Fellows. The twelve apostles they were not.

The result of this Declaration of Independence from the Church allowed ND and other "Catholic" universities to snuggle their secular-seeking snouts up to the trough of federal and state funding. The Golden Dome was dethroned by the Golden Calf. The hallowed Grotto of Our Lady became just one of many campus religious "icons" to hoodwink thousands of autumn weekend visitors into believing that Notre Dame was "Catholic." While some one hundred million dollars now flowed annually from taxpayer pocketbooks into the university coffers.

Almost unnoticed, Notre Dame with its skewed but increasingly insatiable appetite for secular approval—i.e., attendant handouts from the government—had become a microcosm of our nation's capital. As one of my former teachers confided, "Josh, the university seems to be in lockstep with the Marxist leanings of the president and that circle of felons and zany czars who surround him."

"Dangerously zany," I replied. "El Baba and his forty thieves."

By the turn of the century, traditional Catholic values on campus—for which most parents were then shelling out some thirty thousand dollars per year—had become as hard to find as stadium parking places had been in ND's glory days. (I was thrilled that I departed before having to pony up yet another two thousand dollars increase later that year after my graduation.)

To many, the incense in the campus Sacred Heart Basilica had begun to smell like marijuana. Disputes and personality clashes divided Sacred Heart parish leaders. Cracks the width of the Indiana Toll Road split ND's reputation as a keeper of the Faith. Had the patriarch of the Holy Cross Order, the Blessed Basil Anthony Moreau, descended on campus, he would have cried out *"Sacre bleu!"* But most of us were too unsuspecting, or too preoccupied, or too judicious to confront it immediately.

I was a novice assistant in Sports Info, Media Relations, and still dazed that I'd even been hired. So I stood on the sidelines and wondered what my Dad would have said about it all. The vines of secularism—flourishing for decades—were quietly ensnarling themselves around almost all aspects of campus life. Notre Dame had become a disorderly venue for radical liberalism, socialistic political thought, and even pornographic theater that made Chicago's old Minsky's burlesque look like the *Passion Play*. "Sexuality and the human body" became the catchword of not a few coeds. More than 50 percent of them unabashedly acknowledged having casual premarital "hook-ups." Three out of every ten incoming freshmen were pro-choicers.

Alternative life styles were encouraged and the university bankrolled a group of students to fly to Washington and promote a "gay rights" assemblage. (Gay. A word once a classic part of Christmas card greetings, now dropped from many vocabularies.) Only a few months later, ND hosted a pro-homosexual Propaganda Week. Every week was "Anything Goes" and "Let's Misbehave" Week.

Indecision and an arrogant indifference among university leaders compounded the mix. From high-ranking mucky-mucks under the Dome there came not only acquiescence, but worse. In a final-straw move that provoked an international firestorm of outrage among Church leaders—and among much of the Notre Dame family—university president Reverend Henry Ignatius Pankey invited President El Baba, a vocal pro-choicer and acknowledged champion of embryonic stem-cell research and third trimester abortions, to speak at May 2009 Commencement ceremonies. A man who would condemn to death a baby that had survived a botched abortion.

To twist the knife (and ignoring the prescribed counsel of Diocesan Bishop Joseph Tighe), Father Pankey decreed that ND would bestow an honorary Doctor of Laws upon El Baba. A number of graduates and their supporters fought the good fight and turned their backs on the celebratory rite of passage that they'd labored for the past four years. They skipped the ceremony and prayed at Our Lady's Grotto, the 113-year old vault and sanctuary of true Catholicism on campus to those who understood.

Reaction of the faculty (now less than 50 percent Catholic) was tepid at best. A few whimpered, then remembered tenure issues, rolled over, and played dead. Others heralded the upcoming event with raised fists. A brave few stood their ground and let their disapproval be known. The only member of Father Pankey's administration to openly protest, a highly regarded 20-year veteran and associate vice president at ND, was summarily dismissed under the guise of a "restructuring."

Meanwhile, Pankey's mulish refusal to back down only stoked the gathering wrath of other Catholic Bishops and their flocks the world over. His actions and non-actions were a clear rebuff of Pope John Paul II's 10,737-word *Ex Corde Ecclesiae* ("From the Heart of the Church") that commanded Catholic universities to adhere to the Church's teachings on faith and morals. Notre Dame did not. Thus, they failed in their obligation to maintain and strengthen the university's Catholic identity. A stern admonition from the Vatican's prefect of the *Apostolic Signatura* fell on stony ground. There were even outcries from others within the Church hierarchy that the local Bishop (*ordinarii locorum*) demand that the name of the university be changed.

To protest the selection of El Baba and—for the first time in 128 years—a selected recipient of the university's prestigious Laetare Medal declined to appear. The award was cancelled.

I cheered quietly (anonymously and cowardly in retrospect) from the sidelines, not anxious to join the unemployment lines.

On the day in question, Father Pankey introduced El Baba with the obsequiousness of Uriah Heep, all but bowing (El Baba's trademark) and tugging at his forelock.

Student "free-thinkers" brayed like juvenile jackasses in support of El Baba's appearance. *"We are proud to welcome President El Baba just as we have welcomed six sitting presidents before him,"* boldly and questionably announced members of the African Faith and Justice Network, the Anthropology Club, Brazil Club, Campus Labor Action Project, Feminist Voice, Indian Association of ND, NAACP, ND for Animals, ND Environmental Action and The Wabruda, to name a few.

Many alums, meanwhile, turned their framed diplomas to the wall, tossed their class rings into garage drawers, and withdrew their children's admission applications. (The price of two semesters at Notre Dame now topped fifty thousand dollars.) Bequests and donations from the Old Guard began to dry up. ND golf club head covers were exiled to the potting shed, demoted to garden slippers and seed savers. "I'M IRISH" sweatshirts became car wash towels. ND table and floor lamps went for starving artist prices on eBay. "Shame, Shame on Old Notre Dame" T-shirts became a hot item.

I was encouraged to see Web sites springing up overnight like patches of dew, calling for the replacement of "Hankey Pankey" (the sobriquet was inevitable) and for the university to heed the "Catholic" mandate of its charter. Others organized a boycott in alumni annual gift giving. Some fourteen million dollars was almost immediately withheld. It was difficult for more than a few of us to understand how Father Pankey could blithely ignore his responsibility to give public witness to teachings of the Church and the Natural Law.

So I happily followed the example of those Domers, subway alums, and long-time benefactors (some of whom had never set a foot on campus) who aired their angst by slamming their checkbooks shut. The sum of my paltry donations these past ten years would not have reached four figures. But it was the principle.

Added to all was a ripple-down concussion—more like a tsunami—to the university's eight billion dollar endowment. *Cock o' the Walk* university administrators ignored all and appeared to be quite unconcerned with the scandal wrought by honoring the country's most stiff-necked pro-abortion advocate. In effect, they rubber-stamped the university's okay on the culture of death.

This all coincided with the ascendancy of the most corrupt federal administration in U.S. history; a major rupture on Wall Street; a quadrupled federal deficit; draconian new health, business, and "energy" taxes; and a reptilian choking of individual freedoms. The nation was now in the third year of what had come to be known (quietly) as the Baba-lonian Captivity.

The president had shaken off his campaign's charismatic charm like a copperhead shedding its skin. He now tightly controlled both public and Congress with his bully-boy union thugs, "Compliance Camps," total disregard for the Constitution and extra-exorbitant spending.

Muslim mosques in North America now outnumbered synagogues by the hundreds. "America … is a Muslim nation," El Baba crowed from the South Lawn. Most of the nation was outraged, but no one on the Potomac seemed to care.

Meanwhile, my alma mater of two years, Stonehill College, just twenty miles south of Boston (and viewed since its charter in 1948 as no more than a satellite campus of Notre Dame), was attracting an increasingly larger enrollment. One that was also paying a correspondingly soaring price tag to attend. A decade ago, as the new century dawned in Easton, Mass., the future at "The Hill" looked as rosy as the numbers on a Red Sox uniform.

Had one scaled ND's Golden Dome during those days and peered patiently to the northeast—above and beyond the entrenched Ohio and Pennsylvania high school football factories—the relentless rise of Stonehill as a promising collegiate power might have been witnessed.

In the halcyon days after its founding, a football team was probably the last item on the agenda of the CSC priests at Stonehill, not a few of whom had been educated at Notre Dame and then shipped off to nurture the growth of this fledgling college built on the estate of Frederick Lothrop Ames, scion of eighteenth century shovel manufacturer Oliver Ames.

Inevitably, however, it began. At first, they were rag-tag intramural greenhorns bloodying one another on stony, clay fields and calling themselves the Debits, the Blue Bombers, the Crazy Ottos, the Hornets, the Three Monks, the Petunias—and worse.

Theology prof Father Ed Keegan, CSC, at five foot nine and 155 sinewy pounds, was referee, umpire, head linesman, and field judge. Anyone challenging his rulings too boisterously was usually met with an in-your-face, wind-burned nose and torrent of Latin and Gaelic expletives. Losers treated winners—and Father Keegan—to a free beer night at Ma and Pa Twopence's pub on Route 138 down in South Easton.

Father Keegan died before I arrived as a freshman in 1996, but he was a '50s legend at Stonehill. It was said that someone stole his tri-cornered biretta and it became a weekly, pass-along trophy at the pool table in South Easton's Corner Diner.

Eventually, there came several years of encounters with Boston area locals in a Club Sport league. In 1980 Stonehill was one of seven colleges to form the new NCAA Division II Northeast-7 Conference, later the Northeast-10.

An intense program of nationwide recruiting began and now, mid-season 2011, the Skyhawks ruled, topping the Division II poll of the American Football Coaches Association. Their games, to my Saturday afternoon satisfaction, were shown on the Internet's Northeast10-TV.

Skyhawk basketball teams, men's and women's, not only kept pace, but were seemingly unstoppable. It was only a matter of time before chest-swelling thoughts of a Division I membership in the Big East Conference were entertained, however prematurely, on the old 375-acre Frederick Lothrop Ames grounds in North Easton.

Meanwhile, in South Bend, the cumulative discontent with football failures and harshly compromised Moreauvian values was reflected in a conspicuous ebb of funding for the Irish gridders—to a level, it was said, only slightly more than that of women's soccer, men's ice hockey, and a few of ND's other twenty-one lower-profile sports combined.

Costly coaching changes effected no visible improvement. Highly-touted new recruits basked in signing ceremonies, fizzled on the playing field or headlined Michiana police blotters, and then revisited their commitments and went elsewhere. I struggled to make sense of all this in my weekly "Chalk Talk" contributions to the *South Bend Sentinel*.

Inflamed grads, male and female, boiled over. Football woes became the marquee topic for speakers at most of the university's 265 alumni clubs from Maine to Moscow. ND's "new" stadium (a $50 million renovation in 1997) no longer filled its 80,000 seats—and that after 215 consecutive home game sell-outs. Incredulous fans actually found parking spaces within a few blocks of the stadium. Alumni shrugged off e-mail ticket offers from other alumni.

The dismal-to-dire performance of the team gave the school's crusty critics a long-awaited opening. My phone in Sports Info rang off the hook. Spiteful sportswriters with malevolent memories labeled the Fighting Irish the "Sliding Irish." Web sites appeared with such cerebral-challenged titles as "Notre Dame Sucks" and "Jeer, Jeer at Old Notre Dame."

Jokes abounded.

Question: "What do the Irish and possums have in common?

Answer: They both play dead at home and get killed on the road.

None of this made my job any easier.

New grid opponents feasted on our troubles like hungry hounds. Navy, Connecticut, and Utah toppled the once mighty Blue and Gold—and then rewrote their recruiting brochures to tell the world. South Florida avenged championship game losses of its Women Soccer team to ND by thrashing the Irish gridders at home.

Division I regulars Purdue, Southern Cal, and Stanford penciled in a "B for Breather" on their schedules. Big East, Big Ten, and Pac-10 teams competed for late season "cushion" slots against the Irish. Talk of an offer for ND to join the Big Ten and yet retain its lucrative NBC TV contract dried up.

To grads and fans who had lived through the glorious, golden years of Leahy, Parseghian, and Holtz, it was almost physically painful when subaltern Stonehill College was chosen as one of ND's TBA opponents for 2012.

I'd been following the Skyhawks ever since I left New England, and I knew that their chances against the Irish were about as good as my winning the Powerball or Mega Millions lottery. *Somewhat traitorous but honest thoughts for an ex-Stonehill linebacker.*

On a frosty early November morning, the dozen members of our ND Sports Info group crowded together at a small oaken conference table as our boss, Don Hesse, prepared to break the "news" to us. I'd heard it, of course, a couple of days earlier from my friend Ed Wagner at Stonehill. I'd shared it at once. First with my South Bend old-timer pal Mike Meaney, a '52 Irish grad and a treasure trove of trivia from the Leahy era. And then, of course, with the lovely Shelby Lester, my research assistant and heartthrob of almost a year. Now, we were to hear it officially from Hesse, fish-eyed, flush-faced, and fiftyish. And an atheist.

As usual, we were among the last to be told the news. We all braced ourselves. Hesse was a master of circumlocution and usually delivered a message of ten words in several hundred.

For once, the Hessian kept it short as he handed out assignments. I was given two hours to "concoct" (as the glib but non-writing Hesse put it) a release announcing the addition of Stonehill College, North Easton, Mass., to the Irish 2012 grid schedule. Specifically, Saturday, November 3, in South Bend. Exactly one year away.

I'd already written and edited the story in my mind, but I waved one arm slowly to exhibit some interest. "Don, how can Stonehill, a Division Two team in the Northeast-10 Conference, make this leap? Even for just one game? I know that moratorium on moving up to Division One expires next year ... and I know they're probably going to win conference for the second straight year, but ..."

Hesse's protruding stomach rumbled. "Just do it. They're in the CSC family, and maybe they need the cash. Call it President Pankey's prerogative. I'm kidding. Whatever. Whip it up, for God's sake. You're probably closer to Stonehill's sports programs than anyone in the entire state of Indiana. That's your territory up there, isn't it? Your old team?"

"Right," I said. "Born and bred in Sandwich on Cape Cod."

"Now that was bad. Maybe even crumby," murmured Shelby.

Hesse just stared, and then rolled his Grouper's eyes over Shelby and me. "Remember, after fourth-floor approval over in the Main Building—and the AD's blessing here and at SC—we'll still need the NCAA OK ASAP. Chop, chop. Hop to it."

"Right!" Shelby, awash in acronyms, leapt from her chair, slid one shapely leg behind the other and skipped awkwardly over to her computer. I swallowed a swelling laugh.

Hesse opened his mouth but shut it again. For him, there was something terribly erotic about auburn-haired Shelby's one-legged, tight-skirted, inelegant, and in-your-face hop across the room. His two marriages had long ago ended less than amicably, and now time seemed to stand still.

I sat down at my laptop and scanned my notes. Stonehill vs. Notre Dame! It was already all over the 'Net. No mistake. *Hell, we must have been the last ones to be told.*

Said AP: "Who, What to Challenge the Irish?" The "ND Nation" Blog was having a cow: "Stonehill Skyhawks: Stand by to Get Your Wings Clipped!" E-mail cartoons already blossomed, one showing a leprechaun blasting a bird of dubious parentage from the sky with a double-barreled shotgun. Meanwhile, NCAA's site questioned, "Is This Legal?" I just shook my head. *They don't know? They approved it!*

Shelby came over and put her head down next to mine . "You do the whipping up," she stage-whispered to me from under her cascading peek-a-boo hairstyle. "Concoct it. I'm not much at cooking."

Accidentally on purpose, we brushed elbows at precisely the same time. A magic moment. I felt warm all over. *I do love this job. I'd do it for nothing.* I felt like singing.

Chapter 4

In North Easton, MA, at the other end of the eastern time zone, Stonehill College President Father Jake Maloney was chatting in his Donahue Hall office with communications VP Ed Wagner, who had arrived unannounced and was braced against the door frame, looking not all that comfortable. And looking more every day like Captain Binghamton from that old TV series, *McHale's Navy*. Ed fingered his tortoise-shell glasses and raised both hands as though about to pull in a Hail Mary pass.

"Well, Father, what now?"

Father Maloney sat on the edge of his desk. "We did it, Ed. Or somebody did. Never thought I'd see the day. Wish Fathers Sullivan and Bill Gartland were around for this. And Jim Cleary. You know, when I went here, my heart's desire was just to see a Stonehill team wearing real uniforms."

"Maybe we need to have some kind of trophy for this. You know, like the Old Oaken Bucket for the Purdue-Indiana game every year?" He paused.

"How about the Carline Cup? Remember Frank? Graduated late '50s. Coached a powerhouse team in a Boston City league and died, much too young, on the sidelines on Thanksgiving Day. Interesting guy. A dean's list philosophy major here and wound up as a sheet metal worker."

"Father, you'd need something common to us and to ND. What would they know—or care—about a Frank Carline?"

"Well, how about, like, the McInerney Mug? You knew Father Walt McInerney. Died about four years ago but spent a lot of time up here with the CSC mission band. In fact, he was the last of the CSCs who negotiated the purchase of this Ames Estate. And, he spent a lot of years at South Bend as a teacher, a prefect, and pastor of Holy Cross Church. He'd be perfect, don't you agree?"

"Better, Father, better. But forget this trophy stuff. It's not likely, is it, that this will ever become an annual event? Actually, it's damned unlikely."

"I guess so. Well, talked to your counterparts yet out under the Dome?"

Wagner didn't try to conceal his annoyance. "I've got a call in. Actually, two or three. A new guy named Hesse. Bit of a stuffed shirt and not exactly a crackerjack at cooperation. I think I'll forego protocol and call my friend Josh Allen. You remember him. He works for this Hesse now.

"And, no surprise, my phone's going non-stop. Some fool leaked it last night. Our press pals are loving it. Got to get back. They're even making geological jokes about Stone House Hill and the Rockne Memorial.

"You know, Father, we're going to come under the lamp. I wish we hadn't been swept away by the SPC police back in 2003—or whenever it was. I'm sure there's not an Indian tribe in America that would have been offended by a college team called the Chieftains."

"You don't like the name Skyhawks?"

"Not a whit. What else would they be? Landhawks? And we already play another team called the Skyhawks. And another called the Seahawks. And one called the Hawks. And the Falcons. Too damned many raptors. And our logo? A monocled, expectant half-crow, half-fish. A vexed anthropomorphic. Looks like somebody just stepped on its tail or something. And it's not even flying. Just sitting on a nest. Looks like some geriatric seagull straining on a toilet seat. No, we should have left well enough alone. I voted to keep the Chieftains.

"I also wonder how many of those kids on the Student Strategic Planning Committee—and whoever came up with *that* title—knew they were voting for a plane that bombed Vietnam and the Golan

Heights. A formidable and very dependable bird was Ed Heinemann's A4 Skyhawk."

Father Maloney had stopped laughing. "Is that a fact? Well, I didn't know. We won't put it to a vote again. Better not mention that bomber to anyone. Just keep it Skyhawks against the Fighting Irish. Anyway, I voted for 'Shovelmakers.' My second choice was 'Blizzard.'"

Wagner decided to make a clean breast of it. "I love this place, but we're going to get our clocks cleaned. It's a year from today. Our guys are good, but not nearly that good.

"Funny too," he continued, "nobody seems to know we've already had three exhibition basketball games in South Bend. We were massacred."

"But football, Ed. Football! Rockne. Gipp. Miller. Layden. And the Four Horsemen. Loyal Sons! And a sanctioned game. Good Lord. This is going to be fun. Do you need any help? You've already got, what, half a dozen kids down there working for you?"

"Yeah, but wouldn't mind having Matt Sullivan. The senior. The one who edits *The Summit*. He's interned in town with *The Enterprise*. He could be our first line of defense. Give those journalistic jackals a real person to talk to. I'll put something together for your blessing and for Hesse at ND—and, of course, for the NCAA. Which has probably already released something."

Father Maloney, who suddenly realized that his own vainglorious phone calls to clerical pals across the country last night had probably sourced *the leak*, looked the other way. "Get Sullivan. Give him ten bucks an hour."

Wagner, normally more phlegmatic in the presence of his boss, was actually finding it hard not to enthuse shamelessly about this upcoming epic battle. This was truly one for his memoirs. He understood all too well why the media loved it. From now until game day on the third of November 2012, the contest between ND and the obscure Skyhawks was sure to be a mother lode of copy for even the lowliest sports reporter.

Ed could visualize *Enterprise* sports editor Tom Porcari in nearby Brockton savoring the prospect of an all-expenser to South Bend and occupying, with his laptop, one of 330 VIP seats in the stadium's three-tier press box. *Right now Tom's probably feeling neglected,* he thought. *I've ignored both his calls.*

Other campus publicists were energized. Stonehill's WSHL radio tekkies were scrambling to unravel the red tape that would somehow allow them to play a major role. Their calls and e-mails to ND, South Bend, and Chicago outlets had also been ignored. *Stonehill Magazine* artists were already busy sketching prospective covers. And all were wondering who, if anyone, should be connecting with Boston's NBC-TV affiliate WHDH that aired Irish games? Topmost in everyone's minds, of course, was this question: who among us lowlies would be heading to South Bend next November at the school's expense? For the first time, many began to wonder if the local CSCs, like their counterparts in South Bend, had a private jet or two squirreled away somewhere.

There was work to be done. Ed returned to his office and stood for a few moments looking at the framed black-and-white photo on the wall behind his desk. His father, who had worked for John Fitzgerald Kennedy and gone on to become the college's PR man, had snapped it in October 1958. Caught in time. The then Massachusetts senator speaking at Stonehill on the lawn behind Donahue Hall. Standing next to JFK, Father Francis E. Grogan, CSC, Stonehill's registrar in the '50s. The caption beneath the photo: "Massachusetts Martyrs."

Kennedy ambushed in Dallas, 11-22-63. Father Grogan, a passenger on the doomed United Flight 175 out of Boston, 9-11-01.

Ed punched in Dottie's cell number. There'd be no Happy Hour for them tonight.

Chapter 5

The "NDY" Group
Notre Dame, Indiana

Rev. Charles Donahue, CSC, at seventy-nine was the oldest member of the Holy Cross order still to be serving at Notre Dame. At a time in life when most of his peers were checking into Holy Cross House, the last stop for elderly and infirm CSC clerics, Donahue was jogging around St. Joe Lake with a stopwatch, smiling. He was a big favorite with the many students who knew him only by sight.

His fifty-year career had comprised posts in almost all of their way stations on the east coast, the midwest, as far west as Oregon, and abroad. His last assignment at *Notre Dame du Lac* was a respected role in the office of Student Affairs. Father Donahue had friends, all of whom admired the true grit of the man. But there were others in the administration who wished he would just go away. For them, this was a new day for academe and the Church. Time to put all those old school ties and outmoded, intrusive traditions behind.

The El Baba invitation had prompted a calm, reasoned, and highly visible continuum of spoken and published criticism from Father Donahue. The administration was clearly annoyed. They reacted by bestowing on him the title Mediator of the Campus Life Council (CLC). It would have been harder to find a less influential role for the man except perhaps as a secretary for ASTF, the university's Anti-Sweatshop Task Force. The blanket mission of the CLC, like the avalanche of continuing covert and indefinable legislation from Washington, was vague: "provide a forum for students, faculty, rectors, and administrators to discuss matters of Student Affairs."

The administration was well aware of Father Donahue's popularity and also his displeasure with the marked decline of Catholicity on campus. But, they decided, a powerless slot on the already impotent, twenty-five-member CLC might keep him out of their hair. Besides, how much difficulty could a rather docile seventy-nine-year old really pose for them?

But the Reverend Pankey's profanity in honoring President Mubaraq El Baba, the High King of Anti-Life, would not soon be forgotten by Donahue. That was an invitation that would never even have been considered on his watch. And no one knew better than he that Notre Dame had been deeply dishonored. The traditional values and ideals associated with the university were under attack from within—and he welcomed any opportunities to deal with them.

Charlie Donahue had been born in South Boston on the same day that the body of the kidnapped baby Charles Lindbergh Jr. was found. He'd played quarterback for Cathedral High School and loved football. For him, like for Gerry Faust, ND's Head Coach of the early '80s, the ethical caliber of the player was far more important than the score at the final gun.

He was also well-acquainted with Stonehill College and their high-flying football program. He'd spent time there. The prospect of watching them take on the storied Irish made him feel like a teenager again.

Donahue was considered one of the boys to NDY (Not Dead Yet), a small, free-wheeling, Matthau-esque, and unsanctioned club restricted to ND grads who had survived to age eighty and beyond. The NDYers knew Father Charlie well—and what he stood for. Donahue was a man of strict principles and high resolve—and he was not reluctant to take off his collar, if necessary, and prove it.

The monthly Business & Bridge meeting of the NDY club, South Bend Chapter, had convened at Sorin's in the Morris Inn, but it was faltering. At the top of the day's business agenda for these four faithful members was the subject of their close friend Gerry Finn, Class of 1934.

At ninety-nine, Gerry Finn was the university's oldest living alumnus. At the diamond reunion of his class, he stood alone. His only surviving classmate, Marc Haverty, had expired last December in a private plane crash less than a mile from the South Bend airport. Haverty had been making his annual pilgrimage from Frankfort, Wisconsin, to throw flowers on St. Joe's Lake in memory of his long-deceased fiancée Barb McCaffrey, a South Bend librarian and controversial figure on the ND campus in the late 1940s.

Gerry Finn resided in a Chicago condo and NDYers the world over (mostly in Florida) kept in touch with him with large-print letters and telephone. Finn had never waded into www waters. His penmanship was legendary, as was his devoted dedication to the university and to the Blessed Mother Mary atop the Golden Dome. Like that other Gerry, Irish ex-coach Gerry Faust, his first stop on a campus visit was always Our Lady's Grotto.

Finn still served as secretary for all of the classes from '34 through '37 and provided handwritten updates for each quarterly issue of ND's alumni magazine. ("When you have no classmates left around, you improvise…")

A successful accountant before retirement, he was also well-known for making instant calculations without putting pencil to paper. Tell him the last three digits of your Social Security Number and he could successfully multiply that by the last three numbers of your credit card. All in the time it took to hum one chorus of "The Notre Dame Victory March."

Gerry's talents worried his Bridge foes and were admired by his partners. He remembered every card that had been played, who played it, and what "honors" cards in every suit had not been played. It was no mystery why he was still viewed as one of the game's sharpest players and, at his advanced age, he still played competitively.

For his ninety-ninth birthday that very day, November 3, the South Bend NDY group and another gang of Gerry's aging Chicago ND pals (under the banner of Ye Olde Has-Beens) had co-arranged the production of a DVD with video greetings from Gerry's offspring— numbering exactly ninety-nine, including children, grandchildren, and great grandchildren! The DVD would be delivered by two curvaceous cheerleaders from the Chicago Bears in the company of friends and photographers. But that was *this* year.

In exactly 365 days, Finn would turn one hundred and become ND's sole living centenarian among the alumni. The university's network of old timers had yet to come up with plans for commemorating *that* milestone. It had to be something truly exceptional. They knew that Finn had lived to see all of Notre Dame's national championship seasons—and that he hoped to witness one more before joining his classmates on that ageless Elysian field. Until then, however, it was up to his NDY cronies to make his one hundredth a super-spectacular.

Mike Meaney, class of '52 and at eighty-one the youngest of the four South Bend NDY-ers, had, uncharacteristically, taken over today's pre-Bridge banter with a startling revelation.

Next year, he announced, the football Irish would be filling an open schedule slot with Stonehill College of Massachusetts, ND's younger brother in the Eastern Province and an up-and-coming Division II dark horse. What's more, the game would be played in South Bend on Gerry Finn's one hundredth birthday.

Eighty-nine-year-old Wally Whippel grimaced. "Stonehill? Never heard of them. Glory Be to God. Division Two. What next I ask you? How about we get Gerry down here, sit him on the bench, and get our guys to run up exactly one hundred points against these New England newcomers."

Meaney's responding sigh of annoyance turned into a hacking, prolonged cough. He recovered as they all held their breath. "Well, you *should* have heard of Stonehill. All of you. They're in the family. Founded by our Holy Crossers in 1948."

Whippel snorted. "Forty-eight? *Nineteen* forty-eight? Babes in the woods. And what's your source? Who told you this?"

Meaney snorted back. "Young Josh Allen, over in Sports Info. He spent a few years at Stonehill and finished up here. When his Dad was transferred."

Sorin's star attraction, Heidi Symonds, a single blond braid bobbing in time to her provocative pace, honed in on their table. This group of geezers ranked high on her list of favorite customers. And she always had their attention.

"Did I hear someone say Stonehill? And are you kids ready for another? We serve lunch until three o'clock, you know. Lots of time yet. Come on, guys, drink like a champion. Have another …"

Whippel held up his hand. "Please, please, Heidi, none of that 'like a champion' crap. It's lost its magic. In fact, it's giving me cramps."

"Okay, Wally, I understand. What can I get you?"

Lee O'Connor, eighty-five, surveyed her fortyish and still fetching frame. "Wait. You've heard of Stonehill, Heidi?"

"Massachusetts. That's my part of the country, you know, Lee. I have a couple of very good friends there. I know it well. And you guys should, too. They're even paired with ND on Program Double-degree. Three years at Stonehill and two here. You get a Science degree and an Engineering degree. Well, you don't, Mister O.

"Also, Stonehill's head man, Father Maloney, has been in and out of here at least three times since September. Had lunch just last week with Father Donahue. They're old friends."

"Jaysus. So it's Puritan roots you're having?"

Heidi's dark eyes sparkled. "Leave my roots out of this. Tell the truth, I come from the Easty family, a distinguished line of New England witches. Hecate was a great aunt of mine. One of my more reputable relatives, actually. And Stonehill, which you really all should know, is part and parcel of the Holy Cross Fathers' turf. Just south of Boston and a campus as pretty as this one. Prettier, maybe."

"I was getting to that," Meaney exasperated. "This isn't going to be just *any* game. More like a family feud. Patriarch Notre Dame bullying Stonehill— kid brother—or whatever. Junior by a hundred years."

Wally Whippel grunted. "Horsehockey! People in Massachusetts are notorious troublemakers. Always have been. Axe murderers. And they're eedjits. Look at the people they elect. They're batting about one for fifty in the last fifty years. Anyway, why feud with amateurs? Cheeky outlanders." He brushed an ice cube off his rumpled blue corduroy trousers. "Let's order."

Heidi held her pencil and pad at well above her eye level. It was a view they'd all been waiting for and she didn't disappoint.

A second round of drinks followed and heads bowed for a whispered luncheon blessing by Heidi. That brought them to three Reubens with french fries and pickle, and one "heart-healthy" Asian chicken salad for Whippel.

They passed the ketchup bottle around and then glanced furtively at messenger Meaney. How could such a thing be happening? A Division II team they'd never even heard of? Division II? Okay, Irish football fortunes had been on the skids, but that didn't mean we had to stoop to the Little League. What the hell's happened? It ain't the same, this Notre Dame.

"One more thing, guys," said Meaney. "We've already played them in basketball."

Frowns. Grunts. "Not so! When?" asked O'Connor.

"Three times. Once in the '70s, the '80s and just a couple of years ago. All preseason. Exhibitions."

"Who …?"

"We scorched them. But let me remind you all, in case you missed it, there has been more than one suggestion made that we simply take five years off from football and then come back as a Division Two entry."

Loud old-man noises, not all voluntary and not all dinner table-acceptable, ensued.

Meaney changed gears. "Calm down. Anyway, we really need to think of something for Gerry's birthday. Hope our friends treat us with more consideration when we hit a hundred."

"What can we really do but talk about it?" said Whippel.

"We can get Finn's bloody Cubbies to win a Series for him," said O'Connor. "My granddaughter told me there's an account on Facebook called 'October of 2012, Chicago Cubs win the World Series. December 21 of 2012, we all die!'"

"Hey," said Meaney. "Could happen. The World Series part, I mean."

Whippel rolled his eyes. "Right, now let's play Bridge."

Bill Yaworski, at ninety-four the senior of the group and tenth or so in line among all ND grads to blow out one hundred candles, grimaced. "I agree. To whatever."

Class of '40, Yaworski had played guard under ND Coach Elmer Layden in 1939. Now, seventy years later, hair sprouted rampantly from almost every visible part of Yaworski's body except his scalp. Brylcreem hadn't been on his shopping list for decades.

"We'll think of something," he said. "You know, Gerry is world class. Bridge. Played a couple of games with Goren at the Palmer House in the '60s. Let's just keep Gerry alive till next November. And me too while you're at it."

He pushed a deck of cards to the middle of the table. "Draw for deal."

"Wait," said Meaney. "Wait. We're getting sidetracked again. Let's not forget our charter. We did agree to help restore this place to a Catholic university. 'Redeem the times, fill Notre Dame with *real* Catholicism' as Frank O'Malley said. We owe him and Ralph McInerny, Doctor Ralph whom you all knew, more than we can ever repay. He called it, all right. 'The university's vulgar lust to be welcomed into a secular society.'

"Talk about vulgar. Did you guys have the pleasure of viewing that video *We Are ND?* Like drinking a can of 10W-30 oil. A scene from Dante. Half-naked skinheads rolling their bloodshot eyes and leering at the camera and each other. Students! It looked like a pledge party for crackheads. Black Mac would have had them all in irons."

He shook his head. "Well, we did nothing today but have two rounds and roll our cataracts at Heidi. Gongoozlers. Sitting on our butts and watching. Some kind of a self-induced torpor we're in. This should be a wake-up call for all of us. We need to act. Do something. Debate. Communicate. Twitter. All that crap. Get more of the alums behind us. Fight the good fight. I'm sick of ND being laughed at. And I can't believe they didn't get rid of Hankey Pankey. Put him in for another term! How did this bloody happen? Who's next on a Commencement Day program? Charles Manson? Osama Bin Laden? Maybe we could have them both? Manson speaks; the doctorate goes to Bin Laden.

Whippel groaned. "For God's sake, Mike. Quit your twitterin'."

"I'm not through yet. Think of the dimwittedness, the dim-sightedness, the unawareness, the insensitivity of so many of these students. With them abortion is a topic for political debate. A bargaining chip. *See me being adult, See me being socially understanding.* Well, boys and girls, you who are draining your parents' bank account by fifty grand a year, think again."

He slapped his hand on the table. To his NDY friends, this was a new and commanding, but annoying, Mike Meaney.

"We've become a big time embarrassment. A cardboard Harvard with a golden dome. Those Catholic revolutionaries meeting up there in Wisconsin forty years ago. While the world slept. Ensure that ND remains a Catholic institution of higher learning. Something like that, they said. Hell, they did just the opposite."

His voice rose. "We were all too stupid, too apathetic, to see what was happening. A half-dozen college presidents and another twenty of their lackeys, trumpeting that a Catholic university must be free of any external authority, lay or clerical. Pure secularism. Prestige over principles. Remember that? What a betrayal!"

His three friends just stared at him.

"Calm down," said Whippel. "People are staring."

"That was the beginning, don't you guys see? They were protecting our Catholic identity. Well, yeah. That's what they said. Forget Catholic spirituality. Give us research, service and social justice. Crap. Crap. Crap. Pure pretense. It was a schism. No more, no less. They were giving away the store. And it's worse now. Institutional autonomy my foot. The whole point was to get on the state and Fed's payroll. We've become a matchbook university. Notre Dame is no longer significant. Or viable."

"Uhhh, Mike, relax. What are you talking about?" said O'Connor.

"I'm talking about the great Land O'Lakes Rebellion. Up there in white deer country by Lake Superior. A nice little summer vacation back in the '60s. Don't you guys ever read? ND, St. Louis U., Fordham, BC, six—maybe more—Catholic colleges quietly seceding from the Church. Splitting. And agreeing to do whatever the hell they wanted to do when it came to Catholicity. Elitists. We're no longer tethered to the Vatican, they announced quietly. Well, it's time somebody spoke up. We've been hoodwinked all these years."

"Mike, you'll give yourself a heart attack," said Whippel.

"Already had one."

"Come on," muttered Yaworski. "Let's play some Bridge. And screw that Stonehill stuff. Must be some kind of bad joke."

Heidi began gathering up their plates as cards were dealt. Meaney and Yaworski leapt to four spades doubled—and quickly made—dispatching Whippel and O'Connor in the first game. At a penny a point, they were already three bucks to the good. Another win and they'd pocket eight more.

"Deal, deal," loser Whippel growled at partner O'Connor. "And give me something good. More than three points this time."

Meaney, still hyper from his jeremiad, picked up his hand a card at a time. His spirits soared. He winked across the table at partner Yaworski, and smirked at Whippel who was trying to retrieve a card he'd dropped.

O'Connor, dealer, passed. Yaworski passed. Red-faced and grim, Whippel bid a heart. Meaney, holding the heart ace, ten, and four, smiled smugly. "Three no trump," he announced boldly, daring anyone to continue. He played only one convention—and that was Madman Transfer. The bidding, such as it was, ended.

Meaney, now declarer, held his cards against his chest happily and reached for his half-empty glass of pomegranate juice. To his left, Lee O'Connor fidgeted and frowned. At Meaney's right, Whippel stared impatiently across the table at his partner. "Lead, Lee, lead. What the hell are you waiting for? A ruling?"

"He's counting sheep," said Meaney.

Whippel leaned forward. "The County Seat?"

"You need a new battery."

O'Connor gently laid the three of clubs on the table as Yaworski, Meaney's partner and now dummy, began to reveal his cards.

Whippel glared at the offending club lead and then at O'Connor. "Didn't you listen to what I bid?"

"Uh, uh, boys. Table talk," said Meaney, reaching over to cover the three of clubs with the jack. The jack won and Meaney, remembering Whippel's one-heart bid, led the heart eight from the board for a deep finesse. Whippel dropped the five. Meaney, nodding happily, dropped the four and let the eight ride. O'Connor hesitated, and then, to the surprise of all, rose with the heart queen to capture the trick.

Whippel smiled encouragingly. But his face quickly darkened as O'Connor led still another club. As Meaney began to play a card from dummy, to his right came a muffled snarl, a brief bark, then a gurgle, and Whippel's head crashed onto the table, a single drop of blood emerging from his nose. No one moved.

"I guess he wanted me to lead a heart," said O'Connor apologetically. "I didn't have any more."

A young priest leapt from a nearby table and rushed over. Tables began to empty.

Two hours passed before Sorin's reopened. The university and South Bend EMTs had departed, sirens mute. Heidi, red-eyed, scrubbed tabletops.

Later, at his two-bedroom apartment in Holy Cross Village, Meaney, editor of *Indiana Sunset,* a typo-ridden e-mail newsletter for all national members of Not Dead Yet, fired out a special edition informing them of the untimely passing of Wally Whippel, their eighty-nine-year-old South Bend Bridge partner now winging his way to the Pearly Gates.

"Down One," he headlined it.

Wally's funeral was held the following Monday at St. Joe's Church in town. There was a time when Sacred Heart on campus would have been the logical venue, but the Board of Fellows had put a price tag on that. And other benefits. An alum's total donated development fund dollars dictated what privileges would be available to him or her. And Wally, like many others, had stopped writing checks to his alma mater on the day Pankey had invited President El Baba to campus.

It was just as well to bid Wally farewell off campus. Things were edgy. Saturday's loss to Connecticut had left ND fans gritting their teeth and scratching other body parts. It had been Guy Fawkes Day and some yet-to-be-identified villains, in the British spirit of the moment, had invaded the stadium in the dead of night and hanged the coach in effigy from the north end goalposts. Early morning church-goers to Sacred Heart were greeted with the sight of several South Bend police cars, strobe lights flashing, and campus security police officers milling aimlessly about a stadium gate.

It was only the week before, on a Monday Halloween night, that a rock-climbing freshman from Oregon had almost lost his life in an attempt to scale the Golden Dome and attach a brassiere to Our Lady. Never mind it was the 118th anniversary of Father Edward Sorin's death.

"All in Good Fun" heralded an editorial in the student *Observer*. As far as Mike knew, the student was still attending classes, but with one leg in a cast. To Mike, his friends, and most older alumni, it was beyond unthinkable. "He should have his brain in a cast," said Mike.

Six Not-Dead-Yetters had attended Wally's funeral. Only Mike had been physically capable of being one of the casket-bearers. Wally was carried out to an organ accompaniment of "The Notre Dame Victory March." Tears flowed. There had been no overturning the university's decision to deny Wally a mass at the basilica on campus. The extended open palm to rethink the denial had been met with a clenched fist.

Back home after Wally's burial, Meaney pondered his own accomplishments up to age eighty-one. None really, he concluded. Apart from his ND degree in '52 and three years honorable peacetime service in the Marine Corps, he'd simply cakewalked on the cusp of achievement compared to many of his friends.

It was only because of a comfortable pension that he felt he'd never really earned—and a substantial inheritance—that he was able to enjoy the comparative luxury and convenience at Holy Cross Village. But his once quiet (and very pricey) neighborhood was now becoming Vodkaville for more and more off-campus, spoiled juveniles who resented having to actually attend any classes.

Harder and harder to think of these as golden years. He remembered too how angry and betrayed he and many of the Village ND alumni felt when "The Reverend HIPster," Henry Ignatius Pankey, honored the godless Mubaraq El Baba on campus. *All this time later and nothing has changed.*

Meaney also suffered more than a grain of guilt for contributing to Wally Whippel's death.

Ironic. Wally's last earthly Bridge bid was one heart. And his own heart failed him a minute later. I should never have bid three no trump. I only had twelve points. But I had the heart ace, ten and four. Wally had seven of them and six sure winners. He should have opened with three hearts. Lord, Gerry Finn would laugh at the four of us amateurs shaming this game. I wonder if I could have made that contract if he hadn't...

This thing called Death. They all joked about it, but like the buried—though never really forgotten—discretions of their youth, it lurked there in the back of their brains. Well, they'd cheated the actuarial tables for now at least. And whoever survived the longest was the winner, right? And inherits that bottle of Jameson's.

Wally had been the group's Grumpy Old Man. Some still remembered him as being the only member of the campus Italian Club whose last name didn't end in a vowel. They all missed him. Especially Heidi.

He'd died on the Feast of St. Martin de Porres, the first black American saint. He'd been canonized thanks to such miracles as being able to pass through walls, levitate, and converse with animals. *Anyone who could deceive the unwashed masses with such illusions these days would be elected president. Come to think of it...*

Meaney wondered for the fiftieth time what he could personally contribute to Gerry Finn's upcoming milestone. He'd already asked Josh Allen over in Sports Info for help. Josh had met Gerry at a since-forgotten opening day home game and was constantly astounded by the detail the old man could recall from games seventy-five years ago.

Whatever, Mike hadn't been to Chicago in a long time. He'd get up to see Gerry. This week. See how his Bridge games were going. Find out too how the DVD birthday presentation went. And if he'd kissed the two Bears' cheerleaders. Run a picture in the newsletter.

He finally went to bed after one beer and a half-eaten microwaved lasagna dinner. But what to do about Gerry kept him from sleep. He rose before 5 AM, reheated last night's coffee, finished off the last slice of a two week-old apple pastry, and sat down at his aging desktop PC.

"Gerry Finn, Centenarian" he headed a new blank document. Underneath it he typed, "Schedule of Proposed Events." Then he leaned back to think.

It's going to be a helluva party. How can we tie it in with this Stonehill game? Maybe get Stonehill's old guys against our old guys? Wear circa 1920 helmets and play a five-minute, twenty-yard tag game before the kickoff? I like that. And what's the Alumni Association got planned? A birthday cake, I hope. One-hundred candles.

He looked at his computer screen. "Hey!" he said to no one in particular. He was feeling drowsy. He hit some keys. *What about...? About who? The name escapes me.* His head nodded and his fingers rested on the keyboard.

A minute or so later he awoke, blinked, and looked again.

"Osh cdfive Mfrck tht nihtgrdsiuljualitytt=ollqqqqqqqqqqqqqqqqqq
q 22222222222222222222222222222222222222222222222222222
22222222222222222222222222222222222222222222222222222222
2222222222222222222222222222222222 ww"

Right, that's good. Really good. I'm on to something big here.

Chapter 6

The innocently scrumptious Shelby and I connected on **"Free Hors D'oeuvres Night"** in the lobby of the Hampton Inn across the Dixie Highway. Open bar from 5 to 7 and no one asked for a room key. One day, I dreamed, we might actually share one.

It was my birthday and Shelby had promised to buy me dinner at Kildare's Irish Pub. But we had asked Mike Meaney to meet us first.

Shelby tossed her red hair, crossed her long legs and fixed her green eyes on me. "Well, Josh? Your octogenarian pal. Where is he?"

I checked the clock above the door. "He'll be here."

"This Stonehill stuff. It's an opportunity, wouldn't you say? Selfishly speaking?"

"How so?"

"Your time to move, Josh. Cash in on your contacts up there. Face it. The Hessian hasn't a clue. Pretending to edit your release." She rolled her head one way and her eyes the other. "He couldn't write his own obit. Without you, he'd be out of here. Time you moved up. Cultivate all those big dogs. Go for it. You're perfect for this one."

"What do you suggest, Miss Mercenary?"

"Who knows more about it than you? Two years at Stonehill and two more getting your degree here. Time to call in some markers. Maybe you should make a trip back east. Get together with that Boston PR pal of yours, Wagner. Tell them to bring a lot of bandages next November."

"Who needs bandages?" Meaney arrived with a thump, falling rather than sitting into the lounge chair next to us.

"Got to pick up a prescription later, Josh. Let's get at it. Evening, you must be Shelby. The state of Virginia's gift to St. Mary's and now to Notre Dame. Looking even more magnificent than Josh always tells me. Mrrrrowwww!"

Shelby smiled. "Hi, Mike. He said you were a Lothario. Who's your hairdresser?"

Mike snapped his fingers. "I surrender. Just stayin' alive. That's my song."

I laid a piece of paper on the coffee table. "Mike, I've been looking at next year. Some interesting stuff."

Meaney reached for the paper, but I pulled it back. "Wait, wait. Let me read this to you. And sorry about your pal Wally."

"Thank you. We're hoping he'll enlist my guy Michael and a few of the other archangels to ride herd on those troubled and misguided souls over in the Main Building."

I settled back. "Mike, listen. Twenty twelve. A Leap Year. Ever heard of the Mayan calendar? Nostradamus? The Apocalypse? Anti-Christ? That's what we're looking at. Predictions, none gospel, that our world could cease to exist next year. The sun will be aligned with the center of our Milky Way. First time in about 26,000 years. What happens? We'll find out. Work on your cosmic consciousness.

"You've heard of the French prophet Nostradamus? That name, Mike, is just a Latinized version of Notre Dame. According to him, a king-sized comet will arrive in 2012, ending all life as we know it."

Mike raised his right arm and spiraled his index finger downward. "Not a bad idea! Maybe that's what it would take to get El Baba's attention? Or Pankey's? A bit late, perhaps. Anyway, yes, I know about all that wacko stuff. There was even a movie."

"There's more," I said. "The papal predictions of St. Malachy. The destruction of Rome—and the world—during the reign of the Pope who succeeds Benedict XVI.

"None of these, of course, is really anything we can use for Gerry's hundredth, but 2012 could be eventful. Great theater for sportswriters. A comet hitting on the fifty just as we introduce our centenarian. The gods saluting our man.

"And Hildegard of Bingen. A prophetess from a thousand years ago. The advent of the Anti-Christ, she said. *'with ears like the ears of a jackass.'* Sound familiar?"

A young tattooed, lip-studded couple nearby glared and then moved away.

I cleared my throat. "They don't get it either. That charlatan in Washington fools a lot of people. He's the ultimate actor. Really. Should have played the lead in *Titanic*. Then we'd be rid of him. Actually, a midnight bath in the icy North Atlantic is too damn good for him.

"Speaking of which, Mike, 2012 is also the hundredth anniversary of the *Titanic* sinking. All kinds of happenings laid on next April for that. A distant relative of Harland & Wolff, the same company that built *Titanic,* is backing a repeat—and questionably named—'Voyage of a Lifetime' with the cruise ship *Balmoral*. Hopefully without the iceberg this time. Only eleven thousand bucks for a view from the bridge.

"Continuing, before you fall asleep, our next presidential election is November 6, three days after our game with Stonehill. Maybe some possibilities there? Slip a little campaigning in? Launch a few barbs at El Baba on national television?

"What could they do? Hogtie us? Confiscate our Rosary beads? Or maybe drag us down to the South Bend police station, like the friendly ND security guys did to that poor old World War II sub vet and a priest in his '80s. And some nuns and other folks who dared to wear pro-life buttons while the baby butcher was spouting his lies here and contaminating our campus.

"Imagine. Eighty-eight protesters, maybe more, prosecuted for trespassing. Facing a year in jail plus thousands in fines. One set of rules for them; a different one for friends of the university administration. And our Pecksniffian cleric, the Reverend *Pater* Pankey, sitting on the sidelines, saying nothing. How's that for Christian charity? He's turned lip service into an art form.

"Also, Mike, next November will be exactly 170 years since our founder Father Sorin and his brother clerics arrived. If the poor old white-bearded guy showed up today, he'd probably take one look, weep, and Air France back home."

Meaney sat there shaking his head.

"You don't look too excited about any of these."

"You're right, Josh. I'm not. Sorry. And, I forgot to tell you. Our little NDY group has been disinvited from any more Bridge games at Sorin's."

"Wally's heart attack?"

"Nothing like that. Some faculty member—or members—overheard us discussing 'inappropriate' topics. Somebody else complained we were, quote, 'improperly attired.'"

"Pankey's PC Squad. They've probably got your phone tapped. "Anyway, Mike, I took the liberty of calling Gerry Finn and he invited Shelby and me up for a chat. Get to know more about his early life. We were hoping you'd come along …"

"I was planning a trip up there myself," Mike interrupted. "Maybe next weekend. On the train."

"No, no. Forget that. Come with us. Next Monday. I've got to cover the Maryland game this weekend. Lord help us, that game last Saturday made us look like the Breen-Phillips Ladies' Flag Football team. We'll drive up Monday—risk the wrath of the Fed's interstate checkpoints. You can navigate. It's all settled, Mike. Say no more."

Chapter 7

Chicago II

The three of us wore jeans, torn sweatshirts and caps. Mike, in his USMC fatigue shirt from the '50s, wore an earring in his left ear and Shelby had dummy studs on her lips. I was driving "Klunker," our 1988 Pontiac and "second car" that we kept to lubricate our safe passage through federal Eco-Vehicle stations.

We held our collective breaths as marble-eyed, rifle-slinging members of El Baba's National Civilian Security Force (NCSF and known bitingly as "Nasties") backhanded us through without incident into Illinois.

"Chicago hardball," said Mike. "They're out there goose-stepping for a guy who has a defective motherboard. This is still America? We're under siege, for crying out loud. I'm for marching on D.C. with torches and pitchforks."

"Hey, be grateful," I said. "We made it through."

It was reverse racial profiling and it was very, very lucrative for the Feds. They claimed it was done at random, and that only one vehicle per hour was inspected, but everyone knew that if you drove an expensive new car, you were white, and you were well-dressed, your chance of getting handed a color-coded VEV (Vehicle Ecological Violation) sticker was almost a certainty.

It was also well-known that no car had ever been found not in violation following an inspection by the Nasties. The sticker was applied

44

on the passenger-side windshield and there was no known solvent that could remove it. Your first VEV would cost you $100 cash payable on the spot; the second would cost you double and so on up the line. A fine of $1,600 or more was not uncommon, although only a complete idiot would continue to be in violation after being flagged down four times. Of course, if your front plate sported one of El Baba's MB (Muslim Brotherhood) stickers, you were an untouchable. And there were many, many vehicles in the Chicago area that displayed them.

Less than an hour later, we sat on Gerry's palladium-windowed sun porch on the seventh floor of a high-rise just a few blocks west of Lake Michigan.

The day was crisp and the view spectacular through a three-mullioned arch. Gerry's daughter Dorothy, a tall, lean and attractive woman in her mid-sixties, served us coffee. She sat next to Gerry who was wearing sunglasses, a dark blue cap and a white pinstriped baseball uniform shirt with a red-circled "Cubs" over his heart.

"You're late," she told us. "We expected you an hour ago. Dad usually naps about now."

"Sorry," I said. "We had to detour to Michigan City so Shelby could see a rare bird there."

"A Red Phalarope," said Shelby. "On the beach. Actually, there were two of them."

Dorothy's face brightened. "Yes, I know that bird. It's a wader from the Arctic. And it was in Michigan City. Imagine."

"My daughter is a birdwatcher too," said Gerry. "I went with her once. We were where, Dot?"

"LaPorte, Dad. On the lake."

"Right, it was a Ruddy Duck. Don't you love that name? Duddy Ruck. It was caught up in the wind. Going faster than a Feller fastball. Anita Loos said bird life is the highest form of civilization. I'm beginning to believe it."

I'd never heard of her. But Gerry was a wellspring of long-ago trivia.

"Anita who?" I asked.

"Loos, the lady who wrote *Gentlemen Prefer Blondes*. About the size of a bird herself. They made a film of her book when I was finishing high school. No one knows what ever happened to it."

Gerry turned to Mike who was looking admiringly at Dorothy. "Sorry I couldn't get down to campus for Wally's funeral. And after all you guys did for me on my ninety-ninth. I've been meaning to thank everybody. Those ladies from the Bears stopped traffic out in front. I was the most popular guy on the street for a day.

"Wally went the way I'd like to go. At the Bridge table. He was definitely his own man when it came to basics of the game. He'd open with a two-card suit and nine points just to confuse everybody. Did I tell you that I was dealt two successive hands with four aces? If you play long enough, good things happen. Even if you have to wait ninety-nine years. Anyway, Wally will be missed."

"The Mass was in town. St. Joe's," said Mike. "Our pal Pankey closed the basilica to Wally. And to anyone else who's cut off contributions to the university. As you probably know, the endowment is down by a third."

Gerry shook his head. "It's come to that? Rather mean-spirited of the president. I still send a check now and then. Maybe I'll reconsider. And Mike, it's been a long time, but I don't remember you having such a full head of hair. How do you do it?"

"Gerry, when I was at ND, some Polish landscaper used to cut my hair for a buck, a *zloty*. And you sure didn't want to go in there when it was 'Polka Hour' on the radio. You'd come out looking like leftover sauerkraut. After that, I vowed to take better care of it."

Gerry laughed and pulled his walker next to the glider he was sitting on A blue and gold "Fighting Irish" blanket covered the back of it. He leaned forward, head down, one hand cupping his eye. He looked like he was ready to hear confessions. A wheelchair with a ragged beige cushion and a single wheel tilted against the wall behind.

"Well, what's going on with the team? That Maryland game? If you can call it that. We're now two and nine." He chuckled. "I guess we've been spoiled by our history. I was down for the home opener. Mich State. I told Willis, my favorite usher, that it would probably be my last. 'You told me that last year,' he said.

"So what do you suppose has happened to our loyal sons out there on the field? Is it coaching?"

Mike and Shelby turned to me. Only among my close friends was I thought to be an acknowledged custodian of all Notre Dame sports information. Could I explain the sorry plight of the Irish who had performed pitifully against the Terrapins two days earlier?

I just shrugged. "Gerry, I don't think it's all that much to do with talent. Or changing coaches. That obviously didn't work. I think the school has somehow lost its will to win. It's been building. All this political pandering at the top has left the team and a lot of its fans confused. And dispirited. A big price to pay for trying to emulate the Ivy League schools. I don't see it changing soon.

"It's even been suggested that we drop football for five years and then come back as a Division Two team."

Dorothy, who had been quiet, shook her head. "There is nothing that any of us can say or do that will solve that problem. The Dame has had her run for the roses. All I know is they can't start winning until they stop losing. If you ask me, their day is done. For now. So let me hear more about this game with Stonehill."

Mike Meaney had met Dorothy before, but didn't remember her as being quite so engaging. Now he moved his chair closer to the glider and to her. He looked like he was prepared to disclose a national security secret.

"Josh here went to Stonehill for a couple of years. Well, I guess you know that," he said. "It's up near Boston and also belongs to the CSC congregation. They have a pretty fair team, but they're in for whipping."

"Yes, we know Stonehill. But what's Dad's role in all this?"

"Wait," interrupted Gerry. "Don't go making a major event of my birthday. It's not like I actually did anything. Grew old, that's all. I'll be happy just to be around one more autumn."

Shelby and Mike looked at me.

"Well …?" asked Dorothy.

I winced. "He'll probably be introduced on the sidelines. Maybe flip the coin to start the game. Be presented with a plaque at half-time ceremonies. ND's first official centenarian. A new club the Alumni Association launched."

Gerry raised one hand, but Dorothy went on. "That's it?"

Meaney shook his head. "I agree. We need to do better. It's what the Alum group has planned, but I want the whole country to know about your Dad. He's special. At the same time, I want them to know that there are still a lot of people who don't like what's happened to ND."

"The El Baba thing?"

"Exactly. I just don't know how to tie it all together. The game, your Dad, and ND's crumbling reputation. Can you believe now the school's given GE some kind of an award for partnering to sell products derived from embryonic stem cell research? They've lost whatever minds they ever had!"

He fished in his pocket and came up with a sheet of paper.

"Forgive me if I sidetrack us here for a minute or two. My pals think I'm going overboard, but I want to read you something. This is from the Internet. If you search the words *University of Notre Dame*, this is what comes up immediately. It's from an encyclopedia and the exact words—I checked this out—were approved, if not written, by the university.

"'*Notre Dame is a private Catholic research university … whose Catholic character is evident in the many Holy Cross priests serving the school (most notably the president of the university), its explicit commitment to the Christian faith … as well as in campus architecture, especially the Main Building's gold dome topped by a golden statue of St. Mary, a famous replica of the Lourdes grotto and the Basilica of the Sacred Heart, along with numerous chapels, statuary, and religious iconography.*'"

"So, it's '*a private Catholic research university.*' Let's get that up front. Research. Research. The password to the vault in Washington, DC.

"'*Its Catholic character is evident in the many Holy Cross priests serving the school.*' Yes, many. Maybe a total of forty on campus? How many actually teaching? Maybe half. Does it matter? There are 890 lay teachers, less than half of them nominally Catholic. Liberal Catholic at that. The bottom line is this: if you expect your son or daughter to be taught by even one dedicated Catholic priest at Notre Dame, don't hold your breath.

"But wait. One of those forty Catholic priests is, and I quote, '*most notably the president of the university.*' Now that makes all the difference. That's our clean-up hitter. The guy who placed the honorary Doctor of Laws credentials in El Baba's hands. Do we all feel better?

"And did I mention that some universities and colleges have been accused of granting honorary degrees in exchange for large donations? Surely, they wouldn't...

"Continuing with the Internet definition: '*Its ... Catholic character is evidenced in its explicit commitment to the Christian faith.*' Not the Catholic faith, mind you. The *Christian* faith, whatever that is. '*Evidenced ... as well as in campus architecture, especially the Main Building's gold dome ... a famous replica of the Lourdes grotto and the Basilica of the Sacred Heart, along with numerous chapels, statuary, and religious iconography.*'

"So, it should be clear to everyone that all those statues and religious iconography, all that architecture, suffice to make it a Catholic university.

"As far as truly Catholic beliefs go, or its commitment to its mission as a Catholic university? Well, let's not go there."

Mike stuffed the paper back in his pocket. No one said anything.

"We were talking about Gerry's birthday. Sorry to digress."

Gerry raised both hands and waved them back and forth. "Please, no plaque. And no introduction. But I wouldn't mind flipping the game coin." He grinned. "And keeping it."

Shelby turned to Gerry.

"Mr. Finn ..."

"It's Gerry." He winked. "You make me feel like an old man."

"Gerry, we'll do whatever you say, of course, but we need to pull together some publicity on this."

"Understand," said Gerry.

"Josh and I have been trying to find a hook to hang it all on. You know, *This is Your Life, Gerry Finn* kind of thing. So, is there anything in your younger days that attracted you to ND? Your Dad didn't go there, did he?"

"Never knew my Dad. Michael Finn. He died in Ireland a few months before I was born in 1912. A farm accident is all I was ever told. My mom didn't talk about him much. 'The Great Patriot' she called him. I never even saw a picture of him. No, no connection with ND."

He paused. "But, when I was about five, my great uncle, Will Curran, took me to a baseball game. ND and Seton Hall. I remember sitting on the top row of some green bleachers. Almost fell off trying to catch a foul ball. Imagine."

"Where was that?"

"Jersey. That's where my mom and I lived before Manhattan. Then we moved to her sister Nell's apartment. My mother kind of inherited it. My Aunt Nora came over from Ireland and visited us there. And when I turned sixteen—that was 1928—Uncle Will took me to that ND-Army game for my birthday. The one at Yankee Stadium when we won one for the Gipper. Jack Chevigny, who was later killed on Iwo Jima, scored our first touchdown. Do you know the story of Chevigny? Amazing. Bear with me.

"Jack was an assistant coach under Rockne when I started at ND in 1930. He left after Rock died and he became coach of Texas in 1934. His second game was against us. They beat us 7-6. At the end of the season he was given a pen inscribed 'To a Notre Dame boy who beat Notre Dame.' He had that pen with him when he was killed early in 1945 with the first wave of Marines landing on Iwo Jima.

"When the treaty with Japan was signed a few months later on the USS *Missouri*, they noticed the Japanese envoy signing the surrender documents with a pen inscribed in English. You can guess the rest of the story. How it came to be in that envoy's possession no one ever knew."

"That is amazing," I said.

"So your Dad died in Ireland," Shelby interrupted. "Did he ever come over to the States?"

"No, he didn't. He was planning to follow my mother over before the accident. They married in January and she emigrated a few months later."

Shelby and I glanced at each other discreetly. "And you were born in Jersey?" Shelby asked.

"All Souls Hospital, Morristown." Gerry coughed and gave them a hearty, wrinkled smile. "I was always told that the entire medical staff resigned soon after. I never knew if it was a joke."

"Did you play football at ND?" she asked.

"No, no. Baseball was my sport. Josh knows that."

"Ever go back to New York?"

"Just to visit. Right after graduating I got a job here in Chicago. My mom died in '48. Only sixty. She's buried in Queens. Suffered from bad headaches much of her life. I think she'd had some sort of unhappy experience when she was young. Ellie and I visited her as often as we could. Asked her to come live with us. She wouldn't leave New York."

"Ellie was your wife?"

'Yes. She was a St. Mary's girl. A redhead. I was in a summer study class with several girls. I loved them all. But oh, I loved that redhead most of all. She graduated in '34, same year I did and the year Sister Madeleva became president. My good friend Marc Haverty, who died last year, was engaged to Barb McCaffrey, a friend of Ellie's from Chicago. I had another friend, Miriam, a Holy Cross nun. Brilliant. She taught English at St. Mary's when Ellie was there. She's passed on only a few years ago."

"So your wife died, when?"

"1990. We were one of the first couples to be married at Christ the King after it opened in the '30s. Up off the Dixie Highway. We were married fifty-two years. I still miss her. She always said we'd outlive the bottle of Pickapeppa hot sauce we bought on our honeymoon in New Orleans. No such luck. It's still in the kitchen."

"About your mom. Do you have a picture of her?"

Dorothy left the room and returned carrying a worn brown leather box with a broken hasp. Gerry groped through some papers and came up with two faded photos.

"This one," he said, "is mom and me when I was six. She was about thirty. As you can see, I didn't look like an overweight bulldog back then. Now I think I have a wrinkle for every year I've lived."

Shelby, who'd been taking notes, studied the three figures standing on the white-columned, wide front porch of a large stucco country house flanked by huge cedars. "Who's the tall, distinguished-looking guy with his hand on your shoulder?"

"Never did know. Maybe a friend of Uncle Will. That was at Will's home in Somerset County. He probably took the picture."

He handed over a sepia portrait of a beautiful but sad-eyed woman with her dark hair in a waved bob and a string of pearls around her neck. "This was Mom when we lived in Manhattan. Probably just before I went off to South Bend. She would have been almost forty."

"A lovely lady," said Mike, taking the two photos from Shelby. "A shame she can't be here for your hundredth."

"No doubt she'll be watching," said Gerry. "She wouldn't have been surprised. 'You're Thursday's child,' she used to say. Far to go."

"It occurs to me, Gerry," said Mike. "Here we are assuming you'll want to go to the Stonehill game on probably the most momentous day of your life."

"Third most. Don't ever forget my two girlfriends. My two ladies. My wedding day was first and my ND graduation second. Ellie and the Blessed Virgin Mary. My protectors all these years.

"I've probably had fifty people threaten me with parties for next November, but no, I want to be on campus and see that game. I have several clergy friends and Josh who have told me about Stonehill. Dot brought it up on the computer for me. I know the school."

Dorothy had returned the photos to the leather box with a promise to scan them and e-mail them to Shelby. Now she held up a tarnished brass button. "What's this, Dad? Do you know?"

"No, I saw your grandmother examining it a couple of times, but she never told me. I think it was my father's."

"Gerry," I asked, "You told me you knew Rockne, right?"

"Right. I also met his youngest son, Jack, who died a few years ago in South Bend. A real gentleman. Rock was not what you'd call a humorist. A pretty serious guy. I lived in a house on Notre Dame Avenue and we'd pass him occasionally on our walk to campus. 'Good morning, men,' he'd say. Men! 'Good morning, Coach,' we'd respond.

"My freshman year, his last year coaching and the first year in our new stadium, we were national champs. Ten and O. Same record we had in 1924. A guy named Eddie Luther was head cheerleader that year and they gave him almost as much credit as Rock.

"He died in that plane crash the next spring. Sacrifice, dedication, and hard work. That was Rock's golden rule for his players. He could be tough. The priests knew enough to stay away from practice sessions. He'd use language they weren't really accustomed to."

"Days of innocence," said Mike, "compared to what's been going on down there since the late '60s. The campus police blotter these days reads like downtown Detroit. Larcenies, burglaries, rapes, voyeurism, the works. The whole culture of Notre Dame has changed, for the worse, eroded, don't you think?"

Finn hesitated. "I guess I do. Yes. But it's like being a Cubs fan. We live forever in hopes. Anyway, you're talking about days that are gone. You can think about them, reminisce, lament, dream, and weep, but they're gone."

They stayed until Mike noticed Dorothy getting restless. He stood. "I think we've taken enough of your time, Gerry. And Dorothy's. I hope you'll be coming to the annual Alum get-together in June. We'd be happy to pick you up."

"Unless you have a car with a built-in bathroom, better bring an empty milk bottle."

I shook Gerry's hand. "We'll let you know."

"Thank you. It's been enjoyable. There's another class newsletter coming up. I want to get this little visit in print."

Mike held Dorothy's hand a bit longer and stronger than she expected. *Snow on the roof, fire in the furnace,* she thought.

"Joe Swift," said Mike as the elevator descended.

"Who?"

"Joe Swift. Class of 1970. You saw that broken-down wheelchair in the corner. Joe's company makes the fastest motorized wheelchair in the world. 'The Swifty.' Sixteen miles an hour. That's like doing a 1:40 marathon. Well, I know Joe and I'm going to call him. He won't be able to ship a Swifty to Gerry fast enough. On the house, of course."

Chapter 8

The NCSF "Nasties" weren't as obliging this time at the state line. Mother, father and two children stood helplessly by in the cold as El Baba's thugs swarmed over their beige SUV. "Pennsylvania plates," I said. "They probably had no idea."

The stop-and-go return drive back to South Bend took almost four hours. Shelby and I were weary, but excited. Stimulated. We'd been quiet on the trip, but our minds were racing. We stopped briefly when we got off the toll road for some take-out pasta. *Big spender I am.*

We dropped Mike off at his Holy Cross Village home and went on to my one-bedroom apartment where we settled down at the kitchen table with our laptops and linguini. We stared at each other.

Shelby broke the silence. "Let's talk about it. Any ideas?"

"Lots."

"Like?"

"You first."

She looked like she was going to laugh. Or cry. I felt the same way. We were ready to burst. *The enormity! If it were true!*

"A matter of simple arithmetic, isn't it?" I asked. "It's 1912. Gerry's father never comes to the U.S. He dies a few months before Gerry is born in New Jersey in early November. Gerry's mom must have conceived in January or February. In Ireland. Then she comes to the States in the spring."

"Yes. She *and* Gerry, her unborn babe."

"Likely it could have been from Queenstown in April. But there were a lot of other ships crossing the Atlantic to New York. From Southampton, Liverpool, Belfast. And, of course, Queenstown. We need to check out every 1912 sailing and arrival date. All of those ports and more. My head is swimming."

"We don't need to do all that, Josh. Just start with *Titanic*. Passenger list. See who boarded at Queenstown. Probably steerage class."

It used to be so easy, I thought as I booted up my Apple. *In some ways the computer has become the Devil's Directory.* I pressed my right thumb against a small square in one corner of the screen. *Now it's thumbprint, name, birth date and sixteen-digit Federal Registry Code.* Finally, Big Brother spoke: "Approved. Proceed. Browse time starting."

I brought up the complete passenger list. First, second, and then third class. Nothing. Lots of Kates, but no Kate Finn.

"We should have asked Gerry where in Ireland."

Shelby was reading her notes. "Her maiden name. She could have booked passage before getting married. Try Curran. Her Uncle Will Curran, Gerry said. Uncle on her father's side. Bring that list back up. C-U-R-R-A-N I'd guess."

"Bingo!" I said a minute later. "Curran, Kate. Two of them. Two! Both third class. But that's a common Irish surname, Shelby. Let's just search *Kate Curran Titanic* and see what we get."

We got a lot, including a poem from a *Titanic* memorial Web site. A prefaced note identified two Kates as having the last name Curran.

Titanic Duo
Two Celtic Kates signed on to sail
A splendid ship not bound by gale
Nor heavy seas nor fearsome tide,
So advertised the vessel's maiden ride
Both Kates had hopes for richer life
(As someone's nanny, someone's wife?)
They paid their pounds and went aboard
Third class was all they could afford.
The vaunted ship, so trim, so grand
Would squire them to better land.

But too cruel April had its way
Its fog, its ice, its fatal day.
It met the ship in chilling seas
And took its toll with killing ease.

Tipperary Kate, just thirty-five
Not one of those who would survive.
No marking cross there in the gloom
No shamrocks growing on her tomb.
Another Kate, from County Cavan,
Found lifeboat number fourteen haven,
Younger yet, just twenty-two
Her life went on, she'd more to do.
No records tell just where she went
Or what she did or how she spent
Whatever time was hers to spend
Before her story had to end.

They had no privilege, had no fame
Those private two of equal name
Who kept us from our wish to know
Their dreams of all those years ago.

KKC, Cape Cod

"Wow, that grabs you," said Shelby. "*'Of equal name.'* So, *two* Celtic Kate Currans: Kate Curran, thirty-five, of Tipperary, died. Kate Curran, age twenty-two, of County Cavan, lived. Saved in lifeboat number 14. Gerry said he was about six in that photo and his mom about thirty. So that jibes. She was twenty-three or so when Gerry was born. And it's written by a KKC. Could be another Kate Curran!

"Lordy, Lordy, this could be just what we've been looking for. Just could be. You know, Josh, I've had a feeling about this whole thing from the start. I sensed a mystical side to Gerry today. Spiritual. And he's so dedicated to Our Lady. There's a reason why he's lived this long. But we don't know that one of those Kate Currans is really our Kate Finn."

"Records were a bit sketchy," I reminded her. "And she could have booked passage under her maiden name for any number of reasons. We've more than enough to pursue this. Kate Curran, County Cavan. Yes, the age, twenty-two or twenty-three, fits."

"But wouldn't Gerry have known this? At least guessed at it?"

"Could be he just doesn't want the world to know. Or maybe his mom didn't."

We labored at our laptops for another half-hour. Then I mined another nugget.

Name	Age	Class	Ticket	Fare	Group	Ship	Joined	Job	Lifeboat	Body
FINN, Mrs. Kate C.	23	3rd Class	370373	£7 15s			Queenstown		14	
CURRAN, Miss Kate	35	3rd Class	330972	£7 12s 7d			Queenstown			Not Recovered

"Finn! Finn! Lifeboat 14. Oh yes." I was near giddy and Shelby gave me a hasty one-armed hug.

"We'll need more proof than this," I said. "But that pretty much tells it. There were no Finns listed on the first official passenger lists, but looks like somebody figured it out later on. Let's see what else we can find."

It didn't take long. *Titanic* Survivors Death Certificate—Katherine C. Finn (widowed). Issued by the New York City Bureau of Health on July 6, 1948.

I pointed at the screen. "Birthplace: County Cavan, Ireland. Died: 1948. Age: 60. Exactly what Gerry told us. And name of Father: James Curran. And place of death: Queens, NY. She departed Queenstown 1912 and was buried 1948 in Queens. Gerry's mom. 'No bout adoubt it,' as we used to say."

After that, it was easy. Yet another entry surfaced from the Celtic Titanic Historical Society.

Name: Mrs. Kate Curran Finn
Born: Thursday 14th June 1888
Age: 23 years
Marital Status: Married
Last Residence: in Curtrasna, County Cavan, Ireland
3rd class passenger
First Embarked: Queenstown on Thursday 11th April 1912

Ticket No. 370373 , £7 15s
Destination: New York City, New York, United States
Rescued (boat 14)
Disembarked Carpathia: New York City on Thursday 18th April 1912
Died: Saturday 3rd July 1948

"This is huge, Shelby. Gerry Finn will be the toast of the universe. Millvina Dean was *not* the last survivor of the *Titanic* disaster. But Gerry Finn was. Or *is*. We need to find a primary source, someone who can drive the final nail. Indisputable proof. We'll say nothing until we can do that."

"Josh, you realize what a furor this is going to cause? A tumult!"

"Yes, a tumult of titanic proportions. Sorry. But hey, Millvina was two months old and a babe in her mother's arms. Born probably about the same time Gerry was conceived. She was wrapped in a white woolen blanket, put in a canvas bag and lowered into lifeboat number 13. Gerry, in his mother's womb, was into his—what?—second or third month of life as a human being? He was there too in lifeboat number 14.

"And he's still alive. For a reason. Hey, Shelby, life is life and he came over on the *Titanic*. There's no disputing it. If you're pregnant, it's a baby. Do you know a baby can yawn after only eleven days in the womb?"

"When exactly did Millvina die?"

"Two or three years ago. On the ninety-seventh anniversary of the *Titanic* launching, I know that. Not sure of the exact date. They scattered her ashes in the harbor at Southampton. That's where the ship departed from in 1912. At the end, she had to auction off her *Titanic* mementos to pay her nursing bills. So much for government healthcare."

"This whole thing is unbelievable. Interesting, isn't it, the calendar for 1912 is the same as 2012. Listen, why don't we just call Gerry and ask him?"

I said nothing.

"Josh? Are you there?"

"This is something for the ages. I feel like I'm afloat. Maybe not a good analogy. We need some Champagne. We should hang out a

Sleuthing-Done-Here shingle. Can you stay, Shelby? I'll sleep on the couch."

She hesitated. "Not tonight, Josh. Let's regroup tomorrow when we've had a chance to think. Better drive me home while I'm still of unsound mind about all this."

I ate the last of the pasta and washed it down with a coffee cup of milk. Then I sat down at my iBook. I was already past deadline with an analysis of the ND-Maryland debacle. I'd get to that. But today was the first day of something really, really big. And first things first.

Mr. Gerry Finn
240 E. Walter
Chicago IL 60610   *November 14, 2011*

Gerry,

It was very enjoyable, as always, to meet with you today. Shelby and I are most grateful. We thank you for your courtesies—and those of your daughter Dorothy. We also have some interesting aspects of your life's story to pursue with you down the road. We intend to make sure that you receive the attention you deserve in the ND community—and well beyond.

It will be an exciting day when the Stonehill Skyhawks come to town. They have a talented young running back from upstate New Hampshire who might surprise the Irish. Reminds me of Bettis. And he has a great throwing arm to boot.

We look forward to seeing you at the annual June alumni event on campus, but will certainly be in touch again soon.

With Best Wishes, and may Our Lady Mary continue to look after you.

Josh Allen

I hit *send* and it was on its way to Gerry's daughter Dorothy, custodian of the computer at their Chicago abode.

Chapter 9

"We need to take someone into our confidence on this," I told Shelby next day.

"Maybe Mike?"

"Meaney's a good guy, but not sure he could keep it to himself. Let's think about it. We need somebody in the organization who can help us. And who commands some respect. Anyway, bring your laptop over tonight."

It was just after six when she arrived in her new green Prius with a large "everything" pizza and her computer. She winked at me when I opened the door. "Brazen hussy reporting for duty," she said.

"Brazen or not, you're a mind reader. All I have in the cupboard are two cans of beans and some spaghetti. Or …"

"Or what?"

"Or Leftovers R Us. Actually, Shelby, they ate better in third class that last night on the *Titanic*. Corned beef and cabbage. Peaches and rice."

"You've been surfing. I have too. There's a ton of stuff on that ship. Must be thousands of *Titanic* Web sites. More. We've a lot of reading to do. Why was the bow of the ship pointing north, according to those who found her? And did you know Millvina Dean came over on the QE2 in 1998? Visited the house in Missouri where she and her family were originally going."

"I know that her relatives, if she has any, aren't going to be happy to hear she wasn't the last survivor."

"Doubtful there are any. She never married. Should we attack this systematically? Organize our search like normal people do?"

"Well, we seem to be okay with our stumble-and-bumble strategy. We just need to find somebody alive with a second-degree connection to Kate. Maybe in her Uncle Will's family. One of his kids or grandkids."

I booted, searched, and moved along.

"Too many Kates," said Shelby. "Listen to this. That other Kate Curran, from Tipperary? The one who drowned? Her traveling companions were Kate McCarthy and Kate Peters. Here's what Peters, who survived, said: *'I wanted them to come up on deck, but they would not come. They appeared to think that there was no danger. That was the last I saw of them.'*"

I remembered something. "Gerry said his Uncle Will was Newark's City Attorney. Let's follow that line."

It didn't take long. "Listen to this," I said. "Here's Uncle Will. *New York Times*, May 6, 1919. City Attorney all right. William J. Curran. Accompanies Newark Mayor Charlie Gillen on a trolley car but the mayor objects to paying the new seven-cent fare. Uncle Will files a one-penny lawsuit immediately after. The mayor against the railway. Protesting a one-cent fare increase.

"While I'm still here, let me test Gerry's memory again. That hospital where he was born?"

"All Souls, Morristown."

A few keystrokes. "Ho, ho. Shelby. Gerry's up in years, but you can't fault his memory. He was right. *New York Times*. November 30, 1914. Ninety-seven years ago. 'Hospital Staff Resigns in a Body—All Souls needs Changes, Physicians Say.' Somebody had fun writing that headline."

"I think we're getting far afield here," she said. "Too many names and places. Let's close up shop for a bit. Quick pizza break."

We did—but soon returned to our dot gov-timed laptops.

"You bookmarking any of these sites, Shelby?"

She was beaming at her screen and didn't respond. "Try this on for size, my friend. *'Curran & Dunphy, a law firm in Basking Ridge, New Jersey. William J. Curran and David Dunphy. The firm was established in*

1887 by William J. Curran, Esq., grandfather of Mr. Curran and former city attorney of Newark. Contact...' blah, blah, blah.

"Now does that sound promising or what? Uncle Will's grandson. Got to be. A lawyer. With telephone number, e-mail, and all. Too late to call him now, but I'll let you have the honor of doing that tomorrow. He must know something about Kate. She was what, some sort of distant cousin? From County Cavan. Better not even mention *Titanic* to him."

Grandson Bill Curran III was rich in family history, articulate and amenable, but knew nothing of Kate, as we learned when I called next day on a speakerphone. Shelby, in white slacks and white blouse, took notes.

"I was only about six when my grandfather died," Bill said. "He was the patriarch. Spoke Italian, Greek, Gaelic, and Latin. Imagine! Speaking Latin. I know he was born in 1864, married in 1890 and died in 1946. Had thirteen children and five of them died very young. I'm a bit of a genealogy nut. All of his eight children who lived, my father and his seven siblings, are dead now. I know nothing of his cousins or nieces. From Ireland or elsewhere. In fact, it was only recently I learned he was born in Ireland and not the U.S. He was a friend of Douglas Hyde, Ireland's first president, and he accompanied Wilson to Versailles in 1919 for the peace treaty signing."

"Well, his niece Kate—she'd be your first cousin, once removed, I think—lived for a while at his home there in Somerset County. Around 1912 and a few years after that."

"My grandfather," said Bill, "was also the attorney for the diocese of Newark. He often had friends and relatives, clerics, and politicians from Newark visiting at Clairvaux Manor. His second home it was. Two-hundred-and-fifty acres. There were as many as a dozen or more people living there. One weekend, some 3,000 members of the Greek Ruthenian church stayed. In tents. The house is still standing and, actually, it's just a few miles from my office. So tell me. What is it exactly that you're looking for?"

I drummed my fingers.

"We're planning a centennial celebration for Notre Dame's oldest alumnus. Gerry Finn. Chicago. His mom, that's Kate, your grandfather's niece, came over from Ireland. But there's not much documentation. We'd like to find out more about her stay there in Jersey in 1912, thereabouts. Gerry said your grandfather took him to a Seton Hall-ND baseball game."

"Yes, he studied at Seton Hall, like my father and his brothers. Also, the Benedictines and your Holy Cross priests at Notre Dame have had something of a rivalry for a long time. The first Benedictine monastery in America was also founded in Indiana and before Notre Dame, I believe."

"Bill, I'd like to e-mail you a couple of photos taken, we think, at your grandfather's home. If you could recognize anyone, it would be a big help."

"Do what I can. Send them along. You know, if this Gerry Finn's mom was my grandfather's niece, I think that would make him my second cousin. Or something. Wouldn't mind meeting him."

We hung up. "What a good guy," I said. "Hope we don't get a bill."

Shelby smiled. "He's quality. I can tell."

Chapter 10

Stonehill College

Compared to Notre Dame, the oldest of Stonehill College's more than 20,000 alums were still in swaddling clothes.

Lou Gasparini, a World War II Navy vet from the Bronx and member of the 'Hill's first graduating class (1952), was senior among the living at age eighty-five. None of his class certainly expected to ever reach triple digits. It was all they could do just to open a Samuel Adams while watching the desperado on-again, off-again Sox, Pats, and Celtics on their fifty-two-inch Samsungs.

Admittedly, there was a disjointed association of Stonehill grads whose hopes for a championship NCAA team were resolute, actually above 110 on the Fanatic meter. For lack of a better name, they called themselves The Ames Brothers: a tip of the hat to the former owner of what was now Stonehill property. Gasparini was their leader. Most also kicked in a hundred bucks a year to support the college's Varsity Club.

Not a few met regularly on Cape Cod summer weekends as Massachusetts chapter members of the ROMEOs (Randy Old Men Eating Out), replaying Stonehill's W's and L's over clam rolls and beer.

There were some 13,000 Stonehill grads living in New England. The Stonehill alumni office was only vaguely aware of The Ames Brothers. But Gasparini, retired from his job with electric supplier Cape Cod

Grid, tried to stay in touch with as many as possible. They met, as the spirit and their thirst moved them, to critique their alma mater's football program.

The unofficial forum of public discussion for The Ames Brothers was *The Cave*, an Internet blog named after a teepee-like formation of Pleistocene-age boulders on the southeastern part of the Stonehill campus. It was said to have been a camp for the warring Wampanoag tribe (headed by an Indian named "King Philip") in a seventeenth-century war with settlers.

Since Stonehill's founding on the Ames estate, students had found the cave and promontory of granite boulders an accommodating venue for beer parties and the occasional tryst. A half-dozen weddings had been performed there. ("We're beginning our marriage already on the rocks …" read the invitations for most.)

The Cave blog was quick to trumpet the news of the match-up with ND. "Gird Your Loins, Goliath, the Skyhawks Are Coming" was the running head on its home page.

Gasparini, a widower, wasted no time communicating with his closest pals and making preliminary long-range plans for the weekend of November 3, 2012. It was also the year of their sixtieth class reunion, but that was a trifle compared to the encounter with Notre Dame. It promised to be one game that would once again fill every available seat and SRO in ND's stadium.

Now Gasparini was talking with Stonehill's PR guru Ed Wagner who was enlightening him about other events to be tied in with next year's epic engagement.

"You know, of course, their stadium is a no-smoking zone."

Lou, a familiar face at Boston's First Cigar Café, frowned.

"Also, ND's president has declared it a 'carbon neutral' game, Lou. They do one each year."

"Huh?"

"Global warming. Climate change. Whatever the hell. There will be carbon rally teams," said Ed. "I gave them your name as captain of ours. You'll supervise. You know, like anyone driving to South Bend from Massachusetts should inflate their tires properly. And they should remember to drive 'delicately,' not pressing down on the gas pedal unnecessarily."

Gasparini stared in disbelief.

"Relax," Wagner added, "any automobile carbon emissions can be offset by our recycling programs, conserving heat in our dorms, and exchanging old light bulbs for those new ones. You know, the twisted fluorescents. See? We'll be competing with ND's carbon rally team. You only have to keep track of what we do. And make sure we do it right.

"When you get your team together, Lou, get on the 'net and go to ND's Office of Sustainability Web site. That's green dot nd dot edu. You can sign up there."

Wagner was squeezing his chin tightly to suppress a wide smile. Gasparini, rather than conserving heat, was generating it at the speed of comet Kohoutek. Even his goatee was turning red.

Wagner pressed on. "NBC—you know, they're always big on this green stuff—they plan to call it the CO_2 Bowl."

Gasparini relaxed. He shook his head. "Why do I let you do this?"

"Because you're so trusting, Lou. An exceptional quality for someone from the Bronx.

"Now, this one's true. ND will be honoring your counterpart, their oldest alumnus. Gerry Finn. With a G. From Chicago. Said to be a real gentleman. He'll be one hundred on the day of the game. You'll meet him. And like him, I'm sure. He's originally from New York and his mother is buried in Queens, I think.

"It wouldn't be a bad idea if you called and introduced yourself. I'll give you his number. No e-mail. I'll ask some of ND's older alums to get in touch with you. They call themselves the NDY club. Not Dead Yet."

"Well, maybe they're not, but their football team sure as hell will be come next November third."

"Now, now, Lou. Don't get carried away."

Chapter 11

I sat at a round, slightly wobbly maple table across from Reverend Charles Donahue, CSC, newly minted mediator of the Campus Life Council.

"I won't torture your mind with the details, Father, but a friend of mine and I have, we think, found the eleven-pound diamond. Maybe something better. I've been helping out with Gerry Finn's centennial.

"Ah yes, Gerry. What a guy. The wonderment of life. Go on."

"We talked to him in Chicago. About his early days. Then we did a little, make that a lot, of Internet surfing. It's pretty amazing."

"And …?"

"Only Shelby Lester and I are privy to this. She works with me. We're not even sure Gerry is aware of it. For now, we'd like to keep it from the rest of the world. I thought about telling you in the confessional just to make sure."

"Trust me," he said. "I'll treat it like it's one of your mortal sins."

"It may turn out to be."

He listened.

"Well, now. Very interesting. Rather astounding, actually. I'm amazed no one has connected the dots before now. Let's assume everything you've said checks out. What then?"

"Lots of options. Release it to the media right away, put up a few Web sites, make Gerry available, contact historical societies, universities, government groups, even Woods Hole and the divers on *Titanic*. There's a ton of enthusiasts for that ship. Internet social networks. For many it's a cult and then some. Facebook alone has more than two million fans.

"Or, we could hold it until close to the date, then introduce him at a press conference here. Or in Chicago. Maybe just send out some media teasers and then announce it at the Stonehill game. Leak it to the world. Dozens of ways these days. He'll rewrite history. The media will love it—and hate it. Most of them, of course, liberal anti-lifers, will sneer. But he's a lovable guy. Not a dishonest bone in his aged body."

"Josh, you keep saying 'we.' You and Shelby certainly can't put it out as coming from Notre Dame. If your facts are right, you'll need a lot of help. And proof. Between thee and me, the university powers will snatch this out of your head and hand the moment they learn of it. So stay off the local skyline. Mine would be a voice in the wilderness. You could be disciplined. Even terminated. This is 1600 Pennsylvania Avenue–Midwest. Nothing happens unless it's from the top and it's politically correct.

"Josh, I'm told the alumni group is handling this award program in conjunction with the administration. In conjunction of course, means 'under the nail-studded thumb of.'"

I'd first met Father Donahue during his Stonehill days and I knew precisely what he was saying.

"Right, and it's not exactly a five-star program they have in mind. Not even a two-star. A plaque or something and maybe letting him do the coin flip."

I handed two black-and-white photos to him. "That's Gerry's mom, Kate. That one on the porch is about 1918. She and Gerry when he was six. That's his great uncle Will's country home in Jersey. No idea who the man is. We sent these to Will's grandson in Jersey. A good guy. Lawyer, smart. I didn't correct him though when he said the Benedictines were over here before our Holy Cross priests.

"Anyway, he confirmed that the house in that photo was his grandfather's. He couldn't identify anyone. The other pic, the portrait, is Gerry's mom sometime around 1930. Just before he came to ND.

"Finn's a wonderful man, Father, the epitome of what all ND men once were. And still should be. Putting him in the world's spotlight might just restore some of the university's respectability."

"So what is it you want me to do?"

"Advise us. Supervise us. There will be huge outcry and gnashing of teeth from the NARALs and the NOWs, Planned Parenthood, and the ill-informed, anti-life ilk when this comes out. You can see the headlines: 'A Fetus the Last *Titanic* Survivor?' That sort of stuff. Worse."

"Yes, I can well imagine. And President Pankey would not be pleased."

"President Pankey can …," I began. "This would be a great opportunity. Advertise ND's Catholic character. Defend our values. Be a witness for life. Lay it on the line. Life begins at conception. Period."

Donahue feigned surprise. "Is that so? Well, Josh, you wanted advice. I'm giving it. This administration and the Board of Fellows would never go along with it. They're about as politically correct as they could be. Your job—maybe even Shelby's—would likely disappear."

"I don't care, Father."

"Don't be foolish." He paused. "However, if you can find that third party you mentioned, someone to attest to all this, he or she could be the source. Or any third party. ND would have no say. It would be between that third party and Gerry Finn. And I think it would be smarter to announce it well before the Stonehill game. Soon. Give it plenty of time to build. Besides, you can't keep news like this from leaking. Soon. You need to keep control of it."

"You should have been a PR guy, Father."

Father Donahue just smiled. "Josh, if it happens that you need some time out of the office to pursue it, I'll let your boss know that I might need you on special assignment. My influence is ebbing, but … Don Hesse, right?"

"It is and thank you. You're too good to me, Father."

Chapter 12

In just a few days, Shelby and I had accessed countless Web sites under the watchful and prying eye of netczar.gov. On Friday night Shelby reeled in the Catch of the Week. She'd begun with *"Titanic* Lifeboats."

"A lot of conflicting stuff here. Not just two third-class passengers named Kate Curran. Or who was saved and who wasn't. The spelling of names. Heroes. Villains. Guys in women's clothing.

"And, not nearly enough lifeboats. They say Millvina Dean, the last survivor, was in lifeboat 10. She insisted she was in lifeboat 13."

"I'd have to believe Millvina, wouldn't you? She must know. Even though she never even learned about it until she was eight."

Shelby hit a few keys. "Molly Brown, as in 'The Unsinkable.' Known then as Maggie. Boat number six. Did you know she was from Hannibal, MO? Same state Millvina was headed for. Let's try '*Titanic* Missouri.'"

An hour and two hundred plus sites later, Shelby blinked, pushed back her chair, and raised her arms slowly to signal a touchdown. The Mother Lode. *This must have been how Molly Brown's prospecting hubby J.J. felt when his Little Johnny mine in Leadville laid bare its glut of gold.*

"Wha ..."

"Just shut up. Listen, Great and Powerful Wizard. I think we're in the end zone." She began reading.

"From the Unity, MO Weekly Watch, September 14, 2011: Following is the text of a speech delivered last week by long-time Unity resident Marianne Dolan Jamieson at the opening of a new exhibit at the Titanic

Museum in Branson, MO. The exhibit is dedicated exclusively to the Irish passengers who boarded the doomed vessel in Queenstown (now Cobh), Ireland on Thursday, April 11, 1912."

"My name is Marianne Dolan Jamieson. I am eighty-six-years-young and I have led a wonderful life. I was delighted and grateful several months ago to receive the invitation to speak here in Branson this afternoon.

"And there's more to come. Only this week I have had a telephone call from some enthusiastic, young fellow in Massachusetts asking me to be part of an event there next spring called 'One April Night.' It's a one-hundred-year remembrance of the *Titanic* sinking. I have agreed to participate and will stay with a son who lives in the area.

"My father, Edward Joseph Dolan, was on the *Titanic* and one of the seven hundred survivors. He brought his pipes with him and played for other passengers in steerage. He was a good Christian man and the Lord was certainly in his corner that dreadful night. He did not like to talk very much about it."

Shelby looked up at Josh. "Okay, listen closely now."

"I do know," Shelby quoted slowly, "he also saved a young married lady from County Cavan, close to his home in County Westmeath. He pulled her into a lifeboat that had returned to pick up him and a few others still alive. She was suffering from Paddy's Toothache—that is, she was pregnant—and my father visited her and her little boy some years later. Dad eventually lost touch with her after he and my mother went to Ireland in 1921.

"I was born in 1925 and ..."

Shelby stopped reading. I could only grin. "Shazam! Print that out. Put it in our folder. I think I'm on special assignment for Father Donahue. He doesn't know it yet, but he wants me to drive down to, where is it, Unity, Missouri?"

"We need to call Mrs. Jamieson first. Don't want to scare her off. Hope she has a phone. Now, how about breaking out that bottle of two-buck Chuck you've been hoarding, Josh? We deserve it. And maybe a smooch or two."

I banged my knee against the table leg leaping up.

Marianne Dolan Jamieson

There were very few in the small town of Unity, MO, who didn't know Marianne Dolan Jamieson. The eighty-six-year old widow had put the rural Franklin County community on the map at least three times in recent years.

When the local law (including her son Mike, a detective) had been baffled by a rash of missing house pets, Marianne had urged authorities to investigate the menu offerings of a new Chinese restaurant in fifty-mile distant St. Louis. She didn't mention that on one of her early morning "constitutionals" she had noticed several gentlemen of Oriental descent involved in furtive, predawn activity at a Unity neighborhood warehouse.

After a day or two of Miss Marple jokes at her expense, a St. Louis surveillance team intercepted a Hyundai Entourage van making back-door deliveries of questionable foodstuffs to Ballwin's Din Dong Duck.

The big-city daily sent a reporter out and a national wire service picked up the resulting story ("Unity's First Lady Has Second Sight"). Not to be outdone, the Unity *Weekly Watch* reported that Marianne's talents included more than just nipping cat- and dognappers. She was also a crackerjack Bridge player and golfer, having, at eighty, shot her age.

The crème de la crème was left to a vacationing travel reporter who encountered Marianne one Saturday noon at a rural winery and learned that her father, Edward Dolan, had survived the *Titanic* disaster. He was memorialized as the "elbow piper," an ancient art form. He entertained third-class passengers with Irish nationalistic tunes just hours before the collision. A St. Louis TV station had aired a segment on him about a decade previous, but there was no follow-up.

Marianne was also a poet of some note. She'd had a number of her efforts published, including "Whispers from the Deep," a *Titanic*-related anthology.

When my Saturday morning introductory call came, she was contemplating one more poem to read at the upcoming New England event.

"I wanted to talk to you about your Dad. Is that okay?"

"I'd love it. Come any time!"

We made arrangements. Weather permitting, I'd drive to Unity on the following Monday. I might have someone with me.

Shelby, eyes afire, made her feelings known quickly. "Of course I'm going with you. Meet the piper's daughter. Take notes. It's Thanksgiving week and they owe me ten days vacation. We could leave Sunday. Be back Tuesday."

"That'll work. Stanford game is the twenty-sixth, mercifully, the last. It's out there, so the Hessian will be gone."

"A mini-vacation," said Shelby. "And our first overnight."

I arched one eyebrow and allowed myself a small, suggestive smile. It didn't go unnoticed.

"Dream on," she said. "Twin beds and no hanky-panky. Uhhh, no extra-curricular."

Chapter 13

Twin beds it was on Sunday evening at a small B&B on the banks of the moody, murky, and meandering Missouri River a few miles from the small town of Unity. A Bavarian-accented dinner at an historic landmark restaurant. I wandered along the bank of the river and examined driftwood in the dim light while Shelby showered. Our evening's waitress had been named Kate. Clearly, we agreed, an augury of a successful trip.

I awoke twice in the middle of the night. Once to the lonely wail of a passing freight on the tracks by the river. Then again to the rhythmic roar of someone using either a leaf-blower or a chainsaw. I sat up. It was originating from the bed next to mine. "Hey," I shouted. It stopped.

It was mid-morning when, camera, tape recorder, and laptops in hand, we rang the front doorbell of the small, one-story home on a quiet cul-de-sac. The door opened immediately. A smiling, white-haired, blue-eyed lady, crucifix on a silver chain resting on her flowered, lavender blouse, greeted us. She hugged us both as we entered and a black cat rubbed up against my ankle.

"Call me Mary. Only my parents and the newspaper called me Marianne. Sit here. We'll have some good Irish tea and soda bread and a nice chat. Get down, Midnight, and give my friends a seat." The cat obliged and disappeared under the kitchen table.

"Would you mind terribly if we taped our conversation?"

"Not at all, not at all. Feel free with yourselves."

Tea was served in Belleek shamrock cups with a mound of beautifully browned soda-raisin bread. "I made this last night," said Mary. "It's my father's recipe."

Shelby protested, but briefly. We spread butter on warm, thick slices. "We should have brought something for you!"

Mary shook her head. "Be on with you. I'm happy to finally meet someone from Our Lady's university. My son Michael went to one of your games and said that you needed a mascot for good luck. Something like a ram or a goose. Not a leprechaun. He said if it's a pot of gold that you want, you have only to coach a losing team there and they'll give it to you to go away. Is that true?"

"Well, some folks think so," I said. "Your father was a remarkable man. We've read all we could find on him. He saved the life of that young woman who was expecting, and later visited her and her son. Do you know where that was? Or who she was?"

"No. My mother told me that story. Edward, as I might have mentioned, was reluctant to talk about the details of the terrible night. But he told my mother—and she told me when I was a teenager living in Ireland. She also told me he was a very popular lad among the younger ladies in steerage. He and his pipes."

"Where do you think he visited the girl that he saved?"

"Somewhere in the New York City area. That's all I can tell you."

Shelby, who had been sitting next to a window that looked out on some small shrubs, suddenly shrieked, leapt to her feet, and grabbed her camera.

"This is incredible, incredible! Look, a hummingbird! A ruby-throat!"

Mary looked at me, but I just shrugged. "I've been meaning to take that feeder down," she said. "I was sure they'd all be gone by now."

"That's it, exactly," Shelby said, depressing her shutter another half dozen times. "This could very easily be a record for a late observation of a ruby-throat. At the very least, the latest of its kind to be seen in the state this year. I have to submit this to Cornell. Today. And let the Missouri Audubon folks know. One more star in your crown, Mary. Good things just seem to come your way!"

"Shelby," I reminded her. "Shel-by."

"Sorry," she said, "I got carried away. This is November twenty-first. Who'd believe that little guy would still be hanging around the Midwest?"

She put the camera down, opened her attaché case, withdrew a photo and handed it to Mary.

"This was taken at Kate's uncle's home in New Jersey."

Mary glanced at it and looked up with moist eyes. "Sweet Mary, Mother of God, it's Edward. It's my Da! And that's your Kate? And her son? I've never seen this picture. Do you have another?"

"We do, Mary, and we can't begin to tell you what this means to us," I said. "Yes, that's Kate Curran Finn from County Cavan and her son Gerard, Notre Dame's oldest alumnus. The same mother and child who survived that night thanks to your father. So we have much to talk about now."

"Kate Curran Finn. So that was her name. My mother didn't know. Or perhaps she forgot. Or told me and I forgot. And her little boy is still alive? Do you both know what this means?"

"We do, Mary. You're quick off the mark. That's why we're here. And that's why we've got to keep this our secret for now. So don't share it with anyone right now. If anyone else knows, it will be out there in no time. It's a huge story. And you, Mary, are probably the only person on this planet who can verify it. Our friend Gerry Finn is indeed the last survivor of the *Titanic* disaster."

"I'd love to tell my children and grandchildren. I'll see most of them this week for the holiday. But, as Shakespeare said, I'll 'give no words but mum.'"

She looked at the photo again. "This must have been taken just before my parents were married. My father joined the Army in 1917 and then proposed. My mother accepted. 'Sure, the poor divil's going off to war and I thought I'd never see him again,' she said. He never left the States."

She seemed lost in thought. "I'm sure you both know that one of the most celebrated passengers on *Titanic* was the millionaire John Jacob Astor—and his new young wife, about half his age. She was in a delicate condition, as well."

"Yes," said Shelby. "Actually she was one of about ten other women onboard who were expecting and who survived. We checked them all out. Astor lost his life. His wife had her child that summer. John Jacob Astor the fifth or sixth or something. He died a while back."

Mary paused. "Juliette Laroche," she said slowly. "The only black family on *Titanic*. Well, a mixed marriage. She was another who was expecting a wee one. She and her small daughter survived and her little boy was born later that year, I believe. He'd be the same age as your friend."

"Pretty unlikely he's alive," said Shelby. "I'll check it out. Laroche?"

"Yes. L-A-R-O-C-H-E."

It took only a few laptop minutes. Shelby read it aloud.

"Juliette Laroche, widow of Titanic *victim Joseph Laroche, later returned to France, where Joseph Lemercier Laroche was born on December 17, 1912. Juliette Laroche never remarried and never spoke of the disaster. Her daughter Louise, who was two years old at the time of the disaster, lived to age eighty-eight, dying in 1998. The younger Joseph Laroche died in 1987."*

"So her son died twenty-four years ago. That accounts for them all," I said. "I never knew there was a black family onboard."

"No," said Mary, "and they weren't treated with much respect either, even though Mr. Laroche was a degreed engineer. They weren't even mentioned in early accounts of the sinking."

"There is no one else," said Shelby. "We'd like to keep this our secret, Mary, until we can decide when and how to make it known. It might be a part of the celebration we have planned for Gerry's one hundredth next November. It's the day of a big football game at Notre Dame and all the world watches those games on television."

"I've been invited to a grand event in New England next April," said Mary. "Do you think you could get him to attend? It's being sponsored by the Titanic Historical Society, the official group. Of course, they might not see eye to eye with us on this one. A lot of the world these days seems to think that a baby isn't really a baby. I don't know what they think. A wanderer's legacy?"

I hesitated. "Mary, we'll have to figure it all out. I'm not sure Gerry will want any publicity on this. In fact, we doubt he's even aware. He's never mentioned it. We need to speak with him. So let's keep our cards close to our chest for a while.

"Then again, we also have to consider reality. Gerry has some problems. He's had protracted cancer in his left eyelid. He has difficulty reading. And walking. We're all here on loan."

"God has the day and the hour. He knows all," said Marianne. "'*He knitted us together in our mother's womb.*' Psalm 139.

"I have congestive heart failure and I'm grateful for each day. The meds help, so thank God for small mercies. But I don't always remember to take them. It knocks me for a loop. I'm hoping I'll be able to go to Massachusetts next April. But some days it's hard just to move. I'm up early but by noon I'm knackered. I need a squirt of that oil can, like the Tin Man."

Shelby picked up her Olympus digital. "Mary, do you have any pictures of your Dad that we could photograph?"

She was rewarded a few minutes later with a handful of black-and-whites. "Most of these were taken in Dublin. When I was much younger, of course. These others are my Da, my husband Michael, and I, taken in New York before Michael died and before I came out here."

"Do you have any other mementos we might look at?" I asked. "Anything that belonged to your Dad?"

"I do," said Marianne and she soon returned with a pair of brown Rosary beads and what looked like an old, large black blanket.

"These are all he saved from that night. As I told you, he didn't talk much about it. 'The smell of that ice,' I heard him say a few times. 'Oh, the smell of that ice.'"

She handed Josh the beads. "Those beads are olive pits. And this is what he was wearing. This old woolen coat with the Astrakhan fur collar. That greenish tinge is from the seawater. He and some other men were trying to free a collapsible lifeboat when the ship shifted and threw them into the water. You can see how worn the coat is. He said it's what saved him. It hung on the back of the kitchen door. We called it "The *Titanic*."

Shelby took the coat and held it up. Three discolored brass buttons ran down the front. The fourth buttonhole at the bottom lacked a matching button.

"Hold this a minute, Josh."

She picked up her camera and took several pictures. Then she pointed at the bottom buttonhole.

"Mary, you're missing a button. I think we know where it is."

We said our good-byes and headed into St. Louis and the interstate north.

"Incredible, isn't it?" I said.

"It is. Really. Who'd believe I'd be right there at the exact instant that ruby-throat showed up? Amazing."

I glanced at her, but she wasn't laughing.

Chapter 14

It was easy for Father Charlie Donahue to take time off from his Campus Life Council duties. At the moment, the most critical official agenda items for the group were funding for a new treadmill in Badin Hall, chastising male students who persisted in calling one women's residence hall "the fat girls' dorm" and "determening (*sic*) whether the new Sexual Assault Policy could enable students to practice troubling behavior." *So are they for it or against it? And policy? They have a policy for just about everything now. And that word "enable." Something else spawned by the computer. The opposite of "disable," a word that my computer knows well.*

CLC gatherings were infrequent. Nobody questioned the resolution of "action" items—or lack thereof—from one meeting to the next. Father Donahue's phone rarely rang. His e-mail box generally contained spam from clerical garment purveyors or cartoons from old friends. Many of his collared colleagues found reason to duck into the nearest building when they spotted him on campus.

In his few months on the council, he'd received just one invitation to meet with anyone in the university's administration. No more than he'd expected. He and others who had publicly questioned the honorary doctorate award to President Mubaraq El Baba at last May's commencement, however respectfully, were now deemed *persona non grata* on campus.

So when Josh Allen and Shelby Lester returned from their trip to Missouri with the news that their sleuthing had turned up the eighty-six-year-old daughter of the man who saved Gerry Finn and his mother from *Titanic*'s watery grave, he was grateful for the diversion. He hadn't doubted that Josh and Shelby were on the right track, but he had been skeptical that they would ever locate a primary source, as it were, to confirm their secret. So now the question was how to proceed.

Tuesday morning and Josh and Shelby sat anxiously on a somewhat threadbare loveseat in his small basement office, while Father Donahue called Gerry Finn. Arrangements were made—despite background objections from Gerry's daughter Dorothy.

Father Donahue, Josh, and Shelby would drive up on Thanksgiving morning with a cooked turkey and trimmings for five. Plus a bottle or two of Cabernet red from a Michigan winery. Shelby to be chef and Josh *sous*-chef.

"Dad, I've already bought our turkey. And a bottle of Champagne. I was going to start thawing the bird tonight. I thought we'd just have a nice quiet Thanksgiving dinner together. I enjoy cooking for the two of us."

"You'll like Father Donahue, Dottie. He has a great sense of humor."

"Is that Mike Meaney coming? He was about to propose last time. Gazing so sincerely into my eyes. Clutching my hand like he intended to arrest me."

Gerry laughed. "No, Mike's not coming. Just Father Donahue, Josh and Shelby. They're anxious to talk again. Don't know why."

He picked up a book, its blue and gold cover picturing the celebrated Notre Dame "Four Horsemen" astride their bridled mounts—and each clutching a fat football.

"Are we going to finish this today?"

"We are, Dad. Let me make some more coffee."

Gerry Finn's 20 radiation "treatments" on one eyelid over a period of four months had suppressed most of the cancer, but left him unable to read for more than a few minutes at a time. Reading had been one of his greatest joys. Now he was increasingly grateful for book tapes and for his daughter who read to him several days a week.

Something had been stirring in his subconscious since last week's visit from Mike Meaney and his two young friends. Their questions about his parents and childhood had jarred loose a few small fragments from his memory that he had yet to corral. The large-type letter that he received a few days later from Josh somehow seemed relevant. He wondered what "interesting aspects" of his life they wished to pursue. Well, they'd better pursue them soon. His clock was ticking. He was worn out. Yesterday was Bridge day and he hadn't been able to summon up his usual enthusiasm for an afternoon with his fanatical pals. He and his partner had bid and made a grand slam—worth $40 at two cents a point—but it hadn't seemed all that exciting.

Yesterday had also been Joyful Mystery Day and he'd said his weekly five decades to Mary last night while remembering his very first visit, as a freshman, to the ND campus Lourdes Grotto in the fall of 1930. A black-veiled young girl sat against a nearby sycamore tree, weeping. It was just after dawn and no one else was around. He was reluctant to intrude, but finally walked over to her.

"Can I help you, ma'am?" he'd asked.

She'd shaken her head and said something that sounded like "you going" and looked away. He'd seen that she was wearing some kind of slippers, had two dark braids under the veil and she was a beauty. Gerry had been embarrassed and apologized before walking away. He lit a candle, looked back and puzzled. There was no sign of her and the leaves on the sycamore were shuddering violently, although there was no breeze. Gerry had thought about that encounter many times since. He regretted not finding out who she was.

Today he'd been thinking a lot about his dear wife Ellen, the daughter of German immigrants and gone now for two decades.

I've been blessed by the Lord to have lived these nearly one-hundred years and to have had fifty-two of them with her. I hope in the next life she will have me. She missed out on a lot of cute kids. Twenty-nine grandchildren, sixty-three great grandchildren plus our one son and six daughters. Ninety-nine progeny. Count spouses and our family now is in triple digits.

He dozed. The old disordered dream returned yet again, compressing years into seconds.

I kissed her cold, white lips and told her good-bye just minutes before they closed the casket lid. Somewhere, in another room, there was the tinkling of a piano, and a girl was singing "Embraceable You." I followed everyone into the parking lot, glancing around. Our children? Our grandchildren?

I knew all their names, but could only guess who was who. No one seemed to notice me as I fumbled with the keys to my old Packard Starlight and lowered my arthritic body into the driver's seat.

I'll skip the church. Like some celestial white bird, her spirit had long since departed the body that I had held so close to me—so many times. I thanked God for that. And for allowing me at least this final kiss. See you soon. One of these days.

Meanwhile, I have this last odyssey to make. I don't know what it is, Ellie, but Our Lady has told me. And I promised her.

Dorothy came in with coffee but he was asleep, the book in his lap. She touched his hair lightly and lovingly, and went back into the kitchen.

Thanksgiving morning came, cool, crisp, and sunny. Father Donahue, clad in cassock and collar and at the wheel of "Klunker," was waved through by El Baba's "Nasties."

Jeff and Shelby, arms laden, made it as far as the kitchen countertop before Dorothy took over.

"Thank you and now get in there with those two old guys. You kids aren't going to muck up my office, which is what this is. And lucky for you I didn't thaw the bird I bought. We're going to eat at noon sharp, so whatever it is that you want to talk about, talk loud enough so I can hear too."

She laughed, and then they did.

Father Donahue and Gerry were sitting at each end of a dark-leathered, three-cushion sofa. The Notre Dame logo was embroidered on the middle backrest. Josh and Shelby pulled up their chairs to face them, laptops at the ready. Gerry eyed them suspiciously.

"Let's see," said Gerry. "The last time anyone showed this much interest in me was 1931 when Father O'Donnell reminded me, none too gently, that I'd forgotten to say Grace. So what's this all about? The Irish Crown Jewels were stolen five years before I arrived on this planet, so that can't be it."

"You're getting warm, Gerry," said Father Donahue. "These two gumshoes need to talk to you about the year you were born—and about your mom. It's an extraordinary story and we hope we're not violating your privacy."

"Let's hear it."

Josh took a deep breath. "Gerry, did your mom ever talk about her trip over here in 1912? Like when exactly did she come and how? On what ship?"

"Well, no. I guess I might have asked her when I was old enough to think about it, but no. She never talked about it and I don't think I ever asked. At least I don't remember."

"Gerry, your mother—and you—came over on the *Titanic.*"

Gerry leaned forward in his seat. "What?"

"She came over on the *Titanic.* On April 11, 1912, she left Queenstown, now Cobh. She was one of the seven hundred survivors who arrived in New York on the Cunard Line's rescue ship *Carpathia* on April 18.

"She was pregnant for the first time, so obviously you came with her. Which now makes you, undeniably, the last survivor of the greatest maritime disaster in history. You're an international celebrity-to-be. To say the very least. With your permission, we'd like to let the world know. There will be demands put upon you, many of them, I'm sure, tiring. Lots of phone calls, mail, interviews. And some not to your liking. We can just forget this whole thing if you say so. It's your call."

Gerry said nothing. He blinked, shook his head slowly, and looked up at the ceiling. Finally, he just nodded several times and rubbed his right ear.

"Dottie," he called.

Dorothy had been standing in the doorway, unnoticed.

"I'll get it for you, Dad."

The front cover had once been blue, but now it was gray. Some of the gold lettering had worn away and the faded blue showed underneath. The rectangular sepia picture of the four-funneled ship at sea, glued to the center of the cover, was scratched and stained. The spine of the book had long ago been broken and it was apparent that some pages had once been held together with transparent masking tape.

Memorial Edition
Sinking of the Titanic

Thrilling Stories

Told by Survivors

Dorothy, still standing, opened it and began reading.

"Most appalling Ocean Horror with graphic descriptions of hundreds swept to eternity beneath the waves; panic stricken multitude facing sure death and thrilling stories of this most overwhelming catastrophe to which is added vivid accounts of heart-rending scenes, when hundreds were doomed to watery graves, compiled from soul stirring stories told by eye witnesses of this terrible horror of the briny deep."

"That's just one sentence, all without a full stop," said Dorothy. "Now I'll read what's written on the inside cover. Barely legible. *'To Gerard—from Mother, August, 1930.'*"

"She gave me that when I left for Notre Dame," Finn said. "The book was an original, printed in 1912 just a few months after the ship sank. She told me it was one of those books that used to be sold door-to-door after a major news event. Usually some calamity. I enjoyed reading it, but never put two and two together. At least not then. Dorothy and I have talked about it a few times and wondered if Mom had been on it, but decided that surely she would have said something. And I never asked.

"This book was well-used when I got it. I think there were almost three hundred pages and somewhere along the way I managed to lose about two hundred of them. I let some of my friends read it at ND. I guess I'm not surprised to hear this. How did you manage to find out? For certain, I mean?"

Shelby tapped the top of her computer monitor. "Right here. Not much you can't find on the 'net. Once you get past the Washington Watchdogs. And we confirmed it from a feisty old gal named Mary Dolan Jamieson. She lives down in Missouri.

"She's the daughter of another *Titanic* survivor. One who saved your life and your mom's that night. Pulled her out of the water and into a lifeboat. Edward Dolan was his name. He was a musician. Played the pipes. That was him in the picture you showed us, the one with your mom on the front porch of your Uncle Will's house in Jersey.

"And that brass button your mother saved?" Shelby extracted some photos from her case and handed them to Gerry. "Look. That was her father's coat. Look at that last buttonhole. She yanked the button off when he was getting her into the lifeboat. Dolan's daughter still has the coat and you have the missing button."

"We've read a lot about it," said Josh. "And if your mother never mentioned it, she was just one of many survivors who wouldn't. But they all must have carried the horror of that night to their graves. Your mother was a brave woman.

"There were two Kate Currans on *Titanic*, both steerage. The other one's body was never found. She was older, from Tipperary. Some of the papers show your mom's name as Finn and others as Curran. After all this time, there are still a lot of inaccuracies.

"But we found the official documents on your mother's death in 1948. New York Board of Health. I'll give Dorothy the address for that Web site. So that pretty much cinched it for us. Edward Dolan's daughter wrapped it up when she saw that picture of her father on your uncle's porch. So you're one of a kind in this wacky world, Gerry."

"I could have told you all that," said Dorothy. "Even without this *Titanic* business."

Gerry rested his elbow on the arm on the sofa and rubbed his forehead. "Well," he said. "I guess you can put me down for a yes. Our Lady must have kept me alive all these years for more than a plaque and a chance to sit on the sidelines next November.

"It might sound a bit odd to you all, but I think maybe I've known. Since I was a lad. There was a part of my mother's life where I never dared to go. She was always a private person and that's probably why she wouldn't come live with us."

"Do you have your birth certificate, Gerry?" asked Shelby.

"I do. It's somewhere in my bedroom with a lot of other papers."

"We may need it at some point."

"That's not a problem," interrupted Dorothy, and soon she returned with it. Shelby took it from her, placed it on a table and photographed it.

Gerry leaned forward. "You know, of course, that this whole business will not sit well with a great many people. A two- or three-month baby in the womb doesn't have a lot of rights these days, even in our Church. 'Only a handful of cells,' I heard someone say recently. Can't recall who. Someone believing himself to be an authority said it. He also said something like, I hope I've got this right, if you give a fetus social experiences and good food, it would develop into a human being. It would develop! Have you ever heard such nonsense?"

"It goes beyond discussion," said Father Donahue. "As my granddad would say, 'There's naught so queer as folk.' Anyway, we've given this a lot of thought. There's a reason for everything, and, like you, we believe the Blessed Mother has a purpose for your longevity. Not only is this country in chaos, but your alma mater as well, I'm sorry to say. Its Catholic character has been sucked out of it. You could be its shining star.

"Forgive me a few words from the pulpit, but yes, I'm afraid that shadows have indeed fallen at Notre Dame. The university failed woefully in its basic mission by honoring President El Baba, a man who has consistently denied legal protection to a child in the womb. ND, in fact, seems to have become a microcosm of the cavalier thinking that is so prevalent in the nation's capital. How long will it be, I wonder, before they decide that the presence of Mary at the Grotto is deemed offensive to diverse beliefs? We're in trouble and we need help. If we had a flag we should be flying it upside down."

Father Donahue waved his index finger. "And the damage we've done to others. As Bishop Tighe pointed out, that award to El Baba 'sundered the Church.' The values that ND once represented just aren't there and the university's leadership doesn't seem to care. Their Catholicity has been crumbling for decades. They've devalued the Faith with some confused crusade for a vague Ivy League 'excellence.' A craving for elitism. Hah-vahd, here we come! There's a huge fissure in the Notre Dame family. They've become purveyors of liberation theology. Good Lord, just plain Marxism.

"So this could be an opportunity for the faithful to take a strong stand against those who don't believe that life begins at conception. And Notre Dame could restore some of its lost respectability by publicly supporting that stand. Enough said."

Gerry cleared his throat and wiped his nose. "I understand, and I applaud that reasoning. But from what I've been told, it's very unlikely they would do that. They perceive abortion as some sort of political football, not as the intrinsic evil it is. Never mind that it flies in the face of human nature. You know, Father Charlie, you should be the guy in the driver's seat down there in South Bend."

"I'd rather have red ants in my underwear."

Dorothy looked at Father Donahue. "Your friend Henry Pankey doesn't seem to get it, does he? For all his degrees, his perspective is rather clouded. How do your confreres in the community feel about this?"

"Not good. Not ready, though, to go head-to-head against him and the other Fellows. They're outnumbered. I'm sure someone is already grinding my name off the stone destined for my Holy Cross Cemetery plot. Life at the university these days is something like an unhappy marriage. You're committed to it, but down deep you wish it would go away."

Dorothy retreated to the kitchen and reappeared shortly with a tray, five glasses and a bottle of Champagne. "If I'd known this was going to be such an historic news day, I'd have bought five bottles. It's a momentous occasion and we can't let another minute go by without a toast."

She filled their glasses and stood before them. "To the brave men of the *Titanic*, who gave their lives, for their children and wives. To piper Edward Dolan who rescued my grandmother Katherine Finn and my dearest father Gerard Finn who is, thank you, Jesus, and thank you, Mary, Our Mother, here with us today.

"Hear, hear," said Father Donahue.

"Wish I could," said Gerry.

Shelby blinked and sniffled. Josh smiled widely. All raised their glasses and drank.

After wishbone, cranberry sauce, some Michigan red and good-byes, Dorothy helped her father to his room for his nap, pulled the curtains, and turned on the shower. She gave him another hour and returned to dim his bedside light.

"*Oh Mary conceived without sin, pray for us who ...*" He was still awake, whisper-praying, and not aware of her presence. Then he saw her.

"You sure you want this, Dad? We can tell them to forget it."

"Dot, I have no choice. If it will help things down at school ... They say it will. I think I'm supposed to do this."

He pointed to a spanking new, red-framed power wheelchair at the foot of his bed. "Darn. I forgot to ask them about Swifty. I know they're responsible. They must have seen my old one. Didn't know I had another. I wonder if they'd let me on the toll road with this one. It goes at a pretty good clip."

"We've got to take it out again so you can get used to it. You could race it in the Powered Wheelchair Olympics. You're sure to win the ninety-nine-year-old age group."

"The *Titanic*. Isn't this all the damndest thing, Dot?"

Chapter 15

Reverend Charlie Donahue did not suffer fools gladly. As the South Bend winter of 2011 wrapped its icy arms and diminishing daylight hours around the St. Joe River Valley, he was becoming increasingly nettled with the university administration's indifference to its critics. He was one of a small number of CSC priests who had respectfully voiced their objections in a letter to *Observer*, the campus newspaper, before last May's commencement.

ND President Reverend Henry Pankey had not acknowledged their letter—or any of the more than five hundred others to the *Observer* taking the university to task for awarding the death-dealing El Baba an honorary degree. He had even shown the same disdain for a petition to his office with some 360,000 signatures asking that the invitation be withdrawn. The opprobrium now attached to the Notre Dame president seemed to have no effect whatsoever on him. *Pecksniffian Pankey,* Father Donahue thought. *No, that's too kind.*

Now, at a time when common sense would dictate the offering of some sort of sincere olive branch from the Board of Fellows, the backsliding had intensified and the gap had only widened.

A transparent offer from on high to begin "dialogue" with alienated members of the ND family was seen for what it was: a poorly camouflaged circumvention of the real issue, the indisputable and intrinsic evil of abortion. Nor was there any sign of a university apology, now six months overdue, to Bishop Tighe and others of the Fort Wayne/South

Bend diocese. (Not to mention a *mea culpa* to the U.S. Conference of Catholic Bishops.)

At the same time, the Reverend Pankey's planned participation in a pro-life march on the January Roe-Wade anniversary reeked of hypocrisy. He continued to exclude from his "Task Force" any of the student groups that had fought peacefully and consistently against abortion.

What was not said in Pankey's new "Initiatives for Life" was far more telling than what *was* said. Many immediately saw the remarkable similarity between this and the deluge of doublespeak that continued to regurgitate from the El Baba White House.

Clearly, research and diversity, both académé code names for "How to Increase Federal Funding," were the gods before whom those in command swung the incense-filled *barque* of Peter these days. All else was expendable. A real and challenging education for undergraduates (something once available and rightfully expected by students in earlier times) was no longer a serious consideration. It was now but a trivial side dish to studies abroad, diversity workshops and funded research projects. He thought of his old friends Harry and Rae Donovan whose only son was a 1978 graduate. Now when anyone asked them if he'd gone to a Catholic university, their response was "No, he went to Notre Dame."

It had been a few weeks since the trip to Chicago. Father Donahue was itching for a fight and he decided that the time was ripe. Gerry Finn would become his *cause cèlébre*, but he would move slowly, avoiding any imperceptible icebergs. He would heed his own advice to Josh Allen and enlist the support of that spirited young lady of age eighty-six down in Unity, MO. When the time was right, he would do what he could to help his small team light the fuse and launch the Gerry Finn fireworks that would hopefully rally pro-lifers the world over—and back the stiff-necked ND administration into a corner.

Meanwhile, he would focus on next week's meeting of the Campus Life Council. Paramount on the e-mailed CLC agenda he'd just received was "How to deal with rampant cheating and plagiarism among Business and Accounting majors and violations of the Honor Code among Marketing majors. Encourage integrity?"

Donahue winced. *God forbid that anyone would chastise or discipline the poor dears.*

Number two on the list was "Escalating Student Eating Disorders." *Are they asking how we might increase them? They're going to give me one.* Before he could think further about it, there was a knock on the door and Mike Meaney peeked in.

"Got a minute, Father?"

"Come and sit, Mike. What's on your mind?"

"Gerry Finn called me last night. Told me about this *Titanic* stuff. What a story! Who'da thunk?? I'm wondering why Josh and Shelby hadn't told me."

"What you really mean, Mike, is why didn't I tell you."

"Well ..."

"I sincerely hope you haven't mentioned it to anyone. Other than Gerry, his daughter, and a granny in Missouri, only Josh, Shelby, and the two of us know. Good Lord. How many is that?"

"Not a soul. I wanted to talk to you first."

"Tell no one. No one. It would toss a large and greasy monkey wrench into our plans. And impede a presently sketchy strategy to tell the world we really are, I think, a Catholic university."

"A major objective of mine too, Father. Trust me. My lips are sealed."

"Good. Now I have a favor to ask. Did you know that our friend Heidi is leaving us? Going back east, Massachusetts—of all places—to live with her sister until she can find work."

"Damn. I didn't know. We haven't been back to Sorin's since they shut down our Bridge games. We've been playing at my place."

"Well, this is just before the holidays, and she needs help. Somebody to share driving her van. And a small Haul-With-It. I told her you'd probably be happy to do it. Josh Allen has already agreed. A business trip for Josh to Stonehill. It was in the works anyway. He knows their PR people. So maybe the two of you could lend a hand?"

"Good Lord. Father, I'm eighty years old. Can't see the white lines at night. And why is Heidi leaving?"

"She just said she was losing her sense of humor. I think we all are. I'm thinking she might also have a special friend back there. Anyway, you and Josh can get to meet my friend Father Jake Maloney. Stonehill's prez. And Josh is also a pal of their PR guy, Ed Wagner. They'll need to know our plans for the game."

"Yes, and what are they?"

"To be announced. Mike, if I'm not prying, were you ever married?"

"I was indeed, Father. And blessed with three children who have all done well. Why do you ask?"

"Just curious. I came close myself, but her father was killed in Korea and she felt she should stay with her Mom. I guess the Lord knows what's best for us. Did your wife pass on?"

"After I retired, Father, we moved to the country, but my wife changed her mind about the rural life. Know how she told me? We were driving home from a wedding one Saturday and she began singing. 'Leavin' on a jet plane, oh babe, can't wait to go.' And she did. She's living down in Arizona now."

"Sorry."

"No need. We're both happy and we communicate. The kids give us plenty to talk about. No woman could put up with me for very long anyway. She did better than most would have.

"And, Father, if you want to stop by my place tonight, I'm having Yaworski, O'Connor and a couple of other guys in. Any time after five. We're going to toast the guys and gals who were at Pearl Harbor. Today's their day."

"I'll do that, Mike. Thanks."

Chapter 16

It was the Feast of the Immaculate Conception. Shelby declined my daily invitation to lunch. She eyed me with naked suspicion.

"Do you really think I'm going to spend Christmas alone decorating a Wal-Mart tree while you're motel-hopping across America with that blond bimbo?"

"But you said you were going home for the holidays."

She glared at me.

"Have you been to Mass yet today, Shelby?"

"You know I have and don't try to change the subject."

"You do Heidi a grave injustice. She's had a lot of bumps in her life."

"No doubt. Bimbo bumps."

"Shelby, dear Shelby, I didn't think for a minute that you'd want to drive across the country. I'm sorry. Questionable accommodations, even likely uncomfortable, but I hope you will. Only one motel stop planned. Heidi has it in mind to make this a somewhat leisurely drive. Alternate behind the wheel. Meaney's not a big night driver. You might be pressed into service. But no bird-watching detours of more than two minutes from the interstate."

We made plans the next day. Leave early on Monday the nineteenth and complete the eight-hundred-mile trip to Heidi's sister's home in Dedham by Tuesday afternoon. I would then rent a car. Shelby, Mike, and I would drive to Easton where the college is and drop Mike off at a motel. We'd head for Plymouth where my older brother and his wife now have a home. I called him and asked if we could stay a day or two. He was delighted.

I reflected. From deep within my Catholic Guilt cranial compartment surfaced a repressed (until now) replay of that November Friday afternoon, as a freshman at Stonehill, and my shapely, thirtyish, divorced landlady who lived on the second floor. Her name was Connie and she could have been a sister to that Long Island Connie from the '50s, the pop singer. She'd come up to my third floor digs and knocked on the paint-starved door. Black skirt and yellow sweater. She carried a tape measure and she was talking about new bathroom curtains.

I'd met her at the top of the stairs, overnight bag in hand. I'd been about to leave for home.

"Won't take long, Josh. I just need to get some numbers." She walked down the hallway to the bathroom. "Everything okay up here?"

It was okay and about to get more okay. She stepped out of her shoes and climbed up uncertainly on the toilet seat by the window, reaching impudently above her head with the measuring tape. She wavered and I'd reflexively put my hands on her black-skirted hips.

"Thank you. Don't let go, now."

I tightened my grip. "No rush, Connie." I was prepared to stand there for weeks if necessary. Scent of a woman.

She seemed in no hurry to leave. I invited her to share a can of Franco-American spaghetti that I hastily tossed into an antique black skillet. She sat, back to me, at the chipped, white Formica kitchen table. I threw caution to the winds, turned from the stovetop and squeezed her shoulders gently.

"You're tense, Connie. I think you need a massage."

She looked up at me, stood and reached for my hand.

"Took you long enough," she said. "Mr. Innocence."

I turned off the spaghetti and she led me back to the bedroom, locking the door at the top of the stairs on her way.

Two hours later we rejoined planet earth. She retreated down the one flight to her second-floor apartment. "Who's sorry now?" I warbled after her. She stopped halfway down the stairs, looked back, and laughed. "Naughty, naughty," she said. It was a one-time occurrence.

Now, ever since this trip back to Stonehill had been suggested, I'd found my mind straying. And wondering what had happened to

Connie. She'd be in her forties. I was thirty-two, unmarried, and apparently shameless.

But the Lord seemed to have solved that problem for me and removed temptation. Shelby and I had talked about the holidays. And my trip. Hadn't we? I didn't think she'd want to go along. Emerald-eyed Shelby. I was sure she had mentioned a flight back to Norfolk and Christmas with her family in Virginia.

Now? Thank you, Jesus. Her presence would keep me on the straight and narrow. *What was I thinking?*

Shelby's birthday was that following Tuesday, another sloppy snow day. We went to the old Studebaker manse in town, now known as Tippecanoe Place and one of northern Indiana's finest restaurants. It was once the showpiece home of Clem Studebaker, the company's cofounder, and boasted forty rooms and twenty fireplaces. Our table was dangerously close to one of them. I'd asked for a window seat and they'd obliged. Our view was a cistern-like stone wall below ground level.

"Happy twenty-eighth, Ms. Shelby. You're gaining on me," I toasted her. "I have your present on the back seat of my car, in case you hadn't noticed."

"So when do I get it?"

I was scanning the dinner menu. "When I lure you back to my apartment after our lobster tail. Fresh from the St. Joe River."

"Ughh. I'll have the Indiana duckling, thanks."

"A birdwatcher like you? For shame. Don't you take a birdwatcher's oath or something? Have you no loyalty?"

"Loyalty I have. Also an appetite."

"Did your folks send you a gift?"

"Certainly. And one that I will cherish. Sibley's *Guide to Birds*. It's the birders' bible. And not cheap. That's *eap*, not eep. Mom inscribed it, '*Happy Bird Day*.' Did you know that she wanted to call me Lucy? Today's her feast day."

"I remember. The patron saint of good eyesight. My mother prayed to her when I got a black eye in the sixth grade. She was martyred. Worse. Betrayed as a Christian by her boyfriend because she wanted to be a nun. Had her eyes cut out and murdered."

"Your mother?"

I had to smile. "Saint Lucy. And maybe if you prayed to her you could see more birds."

"My eyes are fine. Remember that little ruby-throat I spotted down there in Unity? Did I tell you he was the latest hummer seen in Missouri this year? And the experts at Cornell have verified that?"

"The year's not over yet. Do you get a prize or something? A golden hummingbird?"

Of course not. It's just the honor. The recognition that I'm an observant person. Aren't you proud of me?"

"Shelby, I'm always proud of you."

We finished our meal and what was left of our bottle of white wine from Duck Pond Cellars in Washington State. I'd told Shelby it was the perfect complement to her Indiana duckling. What's more, at $20 it was the cheapest Chardonnay on the list. We sat quietly watching the logs flicker, spark, and spit in the massive fireplace.

"Look at the size of this room. Did you know this house burned down in the 1880s? Well, not the outside. All stone. Took four years to build it and the fire destroyed most of the interior just a few months later. Mrs. Studebaker suffered terrible burns but rescued her grandson. Gregori did a painting of it. Showed her cradling the boy and running through flames and smoke."

"Gregori?"

"Yes, Luigi Gregori. He taught art at Notre Dame. Some of his work decorates the rotunda of the Golden Dome. And he did the Columbus murals just inside the Main Building. Father Tom Walsh, president of ND at the time, was the model for the face of Columbus."

"So where's that painting you're talking about? Mrs. Studebaker?"

"It was donated to your alma mater, I believe. They turned it over to ND and that was the last anyone saw of it."

"Yet another mystery. Something about this place. The campus. Even Saint Mary's. There's that undercurrent. Another life going on. Not in the present. And it keeps going on. It always feels strongest around the Grotto. What's that word? *Palimpsest*? Strange place. Nobody back in Virginia warned me."

"Yes. Well, Mrs. Studebaker went east somewhere to recover from her burns. I don't think she ever came back here."

"I'd love to see that painting."

"Me, too. Now let's get out of here. I want to make one quick stop at Heidi's. See when she wants to pack up that Haul-With-It."

"Heidi?" Shelby stuck a lovely pink tongue out at me. I wasn't surprised.

"You have duckling on your dentures."

"Not," she said.

I braked across from Heidi's home, glancing only briefly at my carefully and colorfully wrapped gift for Shelby resting on the back seat. Sibley's *Guide to the Birds.*

Ah, well. I'd been so smug. "To Shelby from Sibley." My clever card inscription needed to be replaced as well. The gal in the bookstore said there's a mistake in there anyway. Something about a junco not being a finch. Shelby must know.

We climbed out of the Celica and waited as a car sped by, throwing some brown slush in our direction. *Brown slush. Brown Thrush. It's hell loving a birdwatcher.* After it passed, we crossed the street and stepped around a black Ford Expedition SUV with Massachusetts plates. At the same time, the front door of Heidi's modest frame house opened and two figures, arm in arm, emerged.

I blinked. I hoped I wasn't too obvious. Heidi, yes, that was Heidi, who'd swapped her blond, braided ponytail for some sort of tousled, shoulder-length blond tresses that made her look like a Miss America finalist. She was attached to an older, stocky, clear-eyed guy who might have been a Heisman Trophy candidate—thirty years ago. He looked very familiar. They were both laughing.

They came toward us and stopped. Heidi smiled and stretched both arms in our direction.

"Josh! And Shelby! This is a surprise."

She waved her hand at her friend. "I'd like you guys to meet my friend Paul. This is Josh and Shelby, Paul. The kind hearts who were going to help me drive back next week."

Paul had locked eyes with me and I could only stare back helplessly. The last time I had seen him he was wearing a Roman collar and teaching philosophy at Stonehill. The Reverend Paul Doucette.

He reached out and pumped my hand like it was a tire jack. "Heidi, I should have made the connection. Josh and I go back—what, Josh?—

probably fourteen or fifteen years. He was in one of my classes at the 'Hill and one of my better students. Good to see you again, Josh. Just call me Paul. I've retired from the Cloth."

I was stunned. For a change, speechless. Shelby stepped in and gave Paul a smile and a handshake. She turned to Heidi. "Did I hear you say we 'were going' to help you drive back next week? Meaning now we're not?"

"You did. Paul got here today." She pointed at the black Expedition parked by the curb. "My knight in shining armor. I won't need that Haul-With-It. Hell with it. We'll load up our cars when the time comes and follow each other back east. You guys and Mike Meaney are off the hook. Hey, Josh, I sent you an e-mail."

I finally found my voice. "You're still leaving next Monday?"

"Oh no. After the holidays. We'll be around for a couple of more weeks. Paul wants to visit some friends on campus, we have a wedding to go to, and I'm still trying to figure out who I can trust to rent this place."

"I thought you'd settled on someone."

"That someone turned out to be just a front for a bunch of junior class party animals. No thanks. Listen. I'm sure you and Paul would like to chat before we go. And we'd like to tell you our plans. Maybe you could both come over some time this weekend? Saturday afternoon? Let our hair down."

"I think you already have, Heidi," Shelby said. "And it looks terrific. We'd love to visit with you guys. Saturday afternoon's good. Thanks."

"We need to catch up, Josh," said Paul. "First I knew you were gone was when I didn't see you that fall semester, sometime in the late '90s, wasn't it?"

"Exactly," I said. We shook hands again. My feet were itching to flee. "So. We'll see you this weekend. Got to run. We're celebrating Shelby's birthday tonight."

"Happy birthday, Shelby," they both chorused. We waved and skipped through the slush back to my car. I opened the door for Shelby, ducked into my seat, and we were gone.

Chapter 17

Reverend Pankey was cranky. His highly heralded lecture on ethics at the Corbaci College of Business had not gone well. Despite reassurances to the contrary from his colleagues afterward, it was obvious that more than a few in the audience received his words with less than unchecked enthusiasm. Indeed, the tenor of things at the end of his Q&A session seemed to be somewhat bellicose.

That commencement ceremony still haunted him. He wondered why so many still failed to see the underlying reasons for his actions. Surely change could only be achieved by opening one's self to dialogue. To engagement. That was the key. Nothing would ever get accomplished if one turned one's back on those who held slightly differing viewpoints.

Every day seemed to bring yet another ricochet from the president's visit. He didn't want to hear any more about his poor judgment or how to restore the university's reputation. The trustees, thankfully, understood the situation and had given him a free hand in dealing with those who had flagrantly trespassed on university grounds. Thus, he'd given orders to the campus security police that anyone seen erecting one of those FUOTAWFTWTAU signs ("Forgive Us Our Trespasses As We …"), or even carrying one, was to be apprehended and relieved of his or her student ID. Or, if an outsider, detained.

Moreover, he was not about to back off. There would be no leniency for outside trespassers, whatever their age or gender, who had protested the president of the United States. They were trespassers. Period. The Lord's Prayer and FUOTAWFTWTAU did not enter into it.

He really didn't need this continuing flow of annoyances. Like today's gnat that was buzzing around him. Something silly going on over in the Alumni Association office. A woman in Missouri. More vexing than most for some unknown reason. He didn't know why. And he wanted to know everything that happened on this campus. Everywhere. Just too much to get done. And here it was only a week before he would fly to California for Christmas.

He frowned at young Father Fred Fischer, who had dredged up the driblet of news.

"Who is she? This Jamieson woman? And why does anyone want to make a fuss over one of our alumni having his hundredth birthday? That's happened before, I'm sure. Finn just happens to be the only one still alive. This is a waste of my time."

"I really can't say, Father. I only know she called the alumni office asking for Josh Allen—he works over in Sports Information—and then she started talking about university officials attending some banquet in Massachusetts next spring. A celebration of the sinking of the *Titanic*. Said it might help our image. That's the only reason I mentioned it to you. Probably something to do with the president's visit here."

Father Pankey bristled like a porcupine with psoriasis. It was not acceptable to attach any negativity to the honored commencement speaker El Baba!

"Our image is just fine. Well, you talk to Allen and see what it's all about. I think he's that kid who sometimes sits on the bench with the team. Our image is fine. I'm tired of repeating myself. We've got enough to deal with."

It was the day after Shelby's birthday. Last night's image of Heidi snuggling up to the former Reverend Doucette still played in my mind. Shelby just laughed. It was obvious she was relieved.

"We're all human under the skin, Josh. Do you think their situation is unique? You need to be a little more accepting. Don't worry about it. Would you want to be a priest these days? We'll visit them on Saturday afternoon. They did us a favor. Now we can spend Christmas here. Lots of gifts under a tree. For me. Maybe one for you. You can fly up to Stonehill another time and have your meetings."

She'd also laughed when I confessed that my birthday gift to her was a Sibley duplicate. I gave her the bookstore receipt and she planned to swap it. "Thank you, Josh. Really. You can never have enough bird books."

We were in the office early Wednesday morning, midweek of final exams for students. An unexpected summons from on high came to me via the Hessian's crimson-lipped secretary Polly. "Report to the Main Building." *They could have called me direct.* I'd never met Father Fred Fischer but knew he was somehow a part of Father Pankey's inner circle. I dutifully appeared in his office at the designated hour. The Main Building was the centerpiece of the main and south quadrangles, now listed on the National Register of Historic Places. I knew nothing of why I was there. He told me about the call from Missouri.

"So what's her agenda, Josh? What's going on? Father Pankey is interested."

I hadn't been on campus when the piper's daughter telephoned from Missouri. I was caught off guard and feeling like a freshman—instead of an alumnus and nine-year veteran of the university's Sports Information department.

"Don't really know, Father. I didn't talk to her. I do know it's unlikely that she has an 'agenda.'"

"I wonder why she'd call you."

"I've met her. Her dad knew Gerry Finn's mom back east when Gerry was just a kid. Some of us are helping to pull together a celebration for Gerry's hundredth next year. Same day we play Stonehill. November third. We've talked to her about Gerry's childhood."

"Is Gerry a friend?"

"Father, forgive me, but you're beginning to sound like one of our dictator's National Civilian Security Force guys."

His face reddened. "Sorry," he said. "I've been instructed to find out about this."

I went on. "Yes, Finn is a good friend. A big sports fan. He lives for the Irish and the Cubs. He's a great source of ND football history so I communicate with him from time to time. A lot of us do. I agreed to help some of his old-timer pals drum up festivities for his birthday. What's all the interest in this?"

"We're confused. How does this lady in Missouri fit in? And the *Titanic*? She talked about Father Pankey attending some memorial service. Strange."

"What? No. She's never even heard of Father Pankey. She's eighty-six-years-old and a very gracious gal. Mary Jamieson. She lives in a little town called Unity. Near St. Louis."

"And the *Titanic*?"

"Her dad was one of the *Titanic* survivors. So she's something of a local celebrity. I think he eventually went back to Ireland."

"I see."

"We were trying to find out some more about Gerry's early life when he lived back east. We found her on the Internet. And, forgive me, but I have a ten o'clock meeting with the *Sentinel* this morning."

"Okay, Josh, don't let me keep you. Just one thing. Seems like a lot of trouble to go to just to collect some background on Finn. Why didn't you guys just call her?"

"Nothing like a face-to-face, Father."

"I'm sorry I have to ask you all this. Apparently she mentioned helping our university's image. In those exact words. That's what we were told."

"Father, it's no secret that we've taken some bumps this past year. And this woman's son, who lives next door to her, is a big ND fan." I stood up. "Sorry, I have to go."

He was still seated. "Josh, I don't know. Maybe you shouldn't pursue this anymore. Or even get involved with Gerry Finn's celebration. Father Pankey said some of his friends made a scene over in Sorin's. The alumni office is supposed to be making arrangements for Finn to attend that game on his birthday and maybe even letting him do the coin flip. That ought to be enough."

That put the fat in the fire for me. I wasn't going to agree to any such suggestion, regardless of whoever—in whatever office—made it. So I said nothing, just started for the door.

"Josh, would you let me know if she calls again?"

"Okay, Father," I said with forced cheerfulness. I closed the door with probably more enthusiasm than necessary. He'd been pleasant, but a lifetime of unquestioned deference to the collar was wearing thin.

Father Fischer waited a few minutes before heading reluctantly for the office of Reverend Pankey on the fourth floor.

"Allen's a nice guy, Father," he said. "I'm not positive he understood your concern. It's all very unusual. He met Mrs. Jamieson on a trip to Missouri. Apparently her father was a *Titanic* survivor and knew Gerry Finn's mother."

"Well, that sounds harmless enough. Why did they drag me into it?"

"He says they didn't. A misunderstanding, I guess."

"Well, he should know enough to let the alumni office deal with Gerry Finn. He works for the University of Notre Dame. Sports. He's not paid to drum up publicity for geriatric Gerry.

"Have a chat with Joe Gallagher, Father Fischer. Sports is in his bailiwick. Allen's taking his job too seriously. Or maybe not seriously enough. And we need the alumni office to put some spin on that birthday event. Tell them to show Finn off as rock solid Notre Dame, then and now. Nothing has changed."

He hesitated. "While I think of it, call Gallagher and tell him to send Allen's employee records over. We don't need any more budding malcontents on this campus."

I arrived fifteen minutes late for my 10 AM with long-time *South Bend Sentinel* sports editor Jack Graney. He'd been a faithful ND fan for at least fifty of his sixty-four years and was as depressed as any of us with their fall from grace. ND's basketball team was off to another mediocre start and taking a beating from the Big East powerhouses. The Purcell Pavilion's new "Ring of Honor" notwithstanding, the Irish hoopsters were struggling and ripe for a first-round tournament kick in the pants from a number of smaller schools.

Jack had never gone past two semesters at Indiana University, but he was amazingly well-informed on just about any college and conference. He never pressed me for inside information about our teams but I shared a lot with him. And rarely did he challenge my off-the-wall predictions in my weekly "Chalk Talk" column. Our meetings were usually two-hour lunches that often left me almost optimistic about our team's chances for the coming autumn.

I made it back to the office early afternoon. Shelby was anxious to hear about my meeting with rosy-cheeked Father Fischer.

"Nothing to worry about," I assured her. "I told him Father Pankey wasn't mentioned. Frankly, it's none of their business."

"Well, it worries me. They seem to think it is. And I think it is too. You'd better tell Father Donahue right away. We've sort of enlisted him in this plot. And maybe tell Mr. Finn. And Mike Meaney, of course. Warn them off."

"It's not a plot, you beautiful girl. And we certainly aren't going to forget about Gerry's celeb status—or pass up this opportunity to champion the rights of the unborn. Father Donahue would be the last one to back off. And there are a good number of online pro-life groups who'd be ready and willing—even anxious—to go to battle stations on the issue. They'll welcome this news about Gerry being the last survivor.

"I can't even believe we don't have everyone's support on this. Doesn't our esteemed president have enough to do up there in the Main Building? Sometimes I wonder who the enemy really is. And he should be honoring those eighty-eight commencement protestors instead of prosecuting them.

"But you know, Shelby, if it happens that the university dismisses this news about Gerry, they're only going to make themselves look worse. I should think they'd be grateful to show themselves as Catholic."

"Yeah, well, maybe you should visit the alumni office and find out what the piper's daughter really said when she phoned. They could have it all garbled. Setting you up. And I think you need to cultivate some more friends over there." With that, she began waving her arms wildly above her head.

"Are you all right?" I asked. "Is that the YMCA song you're doing?'

"Close," she said. "Watch carefully. It's the C-Y-A song."

I knew that all colleges face difficulties in keeping track of their graduates. More than a few fade into some sort of vaporous limbo after receiving degrees. But until confirmed as deceased, they remain on the university's "active" alumni records.

While collecting background on Gerry Finn, class of '34, I'd chatted with Jessica, a charming twenty-year employee in the alumni office. She'd been able to give me the numbers I needed right off the top of her head.

"We have some seven hundred 'active' alumni who graduated between 1934 and 1942. Assuming a graduation age of twenty-two—and health good enough to keep them a few steps ahead of actuarial tables—all would now be in their nineties.

"Then there's another thirty-five hundred or so who graduated between '43 and '52. So most of them are over eighty."

Just to satisfy Shelby, I returned to the alumni office late that afternoon and inquired about Mary Jamieson's call. I told Jessica what Father Fischer had said and she shook her head.

"Josh, I took that call. Mrs. Jamieson was very nice. I loved her Irish accent. She said she'd talked to some people in Massachusetts and they were interested in having Gerry Finn attend their *Titanic* event. She said his mom was a friend of one of the survivors. She didn't mention anything about anyone else from ND. Certainly nothing about Father Pankey. We tried to transfer it, but you were out of your office. Don Hesse said he'd let you know."

Hesse had not, but that was to be expected. The Hessian did not see himself as someone whose job was to relay telephone messages.

I thanked her, made my way to Father Donahue's subterranean sanctum, and told him about my meeting with Father Fischer.

He was unruffled. "This might well set the cat among the pigeons. No surprise. Somebody could easily guess what you're up to now. *Titanic*, April 1912. Gerry Finn turning one hundred in 2012. There will be blood in the water and it wouldn't be long before you'll be getting a phone call.

"A pity that Father Pankey's name somehow managed to creep into this. But no great shakes. You and your lady friend and Mike Meaney—and whoever— just need to move your timetable up. Like get thee busy. Map something out. So get your ducks lined up. I'd say you don't have much time. They're not very long-suffering over there at headquarters."

On a dreary Saturday of cobblestoned clouds, a thin rain, and sloppy snow, Shelby and I drove over to visit Heidi and "renegade" cleric Paul Doucette, my former Stonehill prof. We'd have plenty to talk about, especially next year's game with Stonehill. I wondered if we should share our *Titanic* secret with them. *Yes, probably a good idea.*

I'd intended to say nothing about Paul's split with the Holy Cross Congregation, but after a couple of glasses of wine, he brought it up.

"It would take me the rest of my life to explain," he said. "Too many changes to the bedrock of our Faith. And compromising academics. Core curricula watered down to get minority program funding. Standards lowered. Too many trade-offs to political interests. Too many *quid pro quos*. I objected, but no one wanted to hear it. It all took more forbearance, more perseverance than I could muster. It affected my health and my ministry. Finally I'd just had enough.

"I was laicized ten years ago, all according to protocol, and have been teaching in Gloucester ever since. Since then, I've made continuing efforts, without success, to receive a dispensation from celibacy. As you probably know, that has to come from Rome. Unfortunately, my requests have been, well, ignored. Because someone in northern Italy 450 years ago said that this is how it shall be. Ordination is forever. Nonetheless, Heidi and I have stayed in touch and she's finally agreed to be my wife."

Canon law was as much a mystery to me as Pankey's judgment in awarding El Baba an honorary degree. There was so much I did not understand.

"Well, that's great," I said. "We wish you both much happiness. When's the big day?"

"Sooner than you think," laughed Heidi. "Father Donahue is going to marry us at the end of the month. That's the wedding we were telling you about. Ours! Christ the King up on Darden Road. Can you guys make it? Saturday the thirty-first. Three PM and no presents! We don't have room in our cars!"

I interrupted. "Christ the King? Hey. That's where Gerry Finn, ND's oldest alum, got married. They were one of the first couples after it was founded in the '30s."

"Heidi mentioned him," said Paul. "He's famous."

"We'd be tickled pink to attend your wedding," said Shelby. "And we're delighted for you both. Truthfully, we're happy not to be driving east his time of year. And speaking of Gerry Finn, and being famous, we have a secret we'd like to share with you."

And we did.

Chapter 18

Shelby and I had spent Christmas week—and the week after—sketching preliminary plans to tell the world that a ninety-nine-year-old retired accountant in Chicago with failing eyesight was the sole living survivor of the greatest disaster in maritime history. We realized that we'd taken on a monumental, full-time task. And that we weren't experienced or knowledgeable enough about the most famous ship in the world to do this properly. It occurred to us that we'd also need legal help.

Newlyweds Paul and Heidi had departed early this morning for the east coast. A strong overnight west wind had done its usual tricks, scooping up moisture from Lake Michigan and depositing it in the form of heavy snow on northern Indiana, southern Michigan and eastward. Together with a small group of friends from the university, we had bid our friends good-bye and, shivering, showered them—through a veil of sideways, stinging snow—with our leftover rice. Paul, in his Expedition, followed Heidi's ten-year-old brown 4Runner. Shelby, who only last month had referred to Heidi as a "blond bimbo," brushed one hand across her eyes as the couple drove off. I refrained from saying anything.

Our earlier Saturday afternoon "visit" with Paul and Heidi had turned into a post-midnight winging that included some friends who had happened by. It was a side to both that I'd never seen and we went away feeling like we'd known them forever. Their wedding on New Year's Eve had been small, mixed, and emotionally charged. We sat with

Mike Meaney and some of his "Not Dead Yet" Bridge buddies, all of whom knew Heidi well.

She and Paul said their vows in front of a huge Christmas tree adorned with white lights and silver ornaments. Father Donahue, celebrant, was spirited and smiling.

Paul and Heidi had both had been a major help with our secret strategy to introduce Gerry Finn to *Titanic* aficionados and the world at large.

"Rule number one," Paul said. "Don't involve the university or the Holy Cross Congregation. At all. Let them make their award next autumn and whatever else they want to do at the Stonehill game. By that time, anyone in the world who's interested will know that Gerry was on the ship. They can make up their own minds whether he was a fetus or a baby. A baby of course for us, but not to a lot of others."

Later, Heidi had pointed out the obvious to me as far as the mechanics of getting the news out. "Josh, seems to me your pal Jack Graney at the *Sentinel*, however godless it may have become, would like nothing better than to have his newspaper break that story. His publisher would love him. Sounds like you guys have accumulated more than enough evidence. You'd have access to all their facilities and sources. And they've got lawyers. Imagine! The *South Bend Sentinel* scooping those other media munchkins here and overseas. Their first role on the world stage."

"Heidi, I don't know why I never thought of that. Right under my nose. Want my job? Not much excites Jack, but I think this will. It's a local, national, and international story. The story of the century for the maritime world. We can pick our time. We just need to keep it under wraps for a while. Maybe let it go a few weeks before that April affair up in New England. Thank you, Heidi."

Shelby and I knew that a single slip-up could short-circuit even the best-laid plans to keep our secret. I worried too that Gerry himself might forget and say something.

We called Mary Jamieson down in Missouri and told her we might be back to visit.

"We'll announce this probably in March, Mary, so we have to keep it really close until then. We'll try to help you get to the memorial dinner up in New England. We might even have some sort of video hookup with Gerry Finn in Chicago that night. He won't be able to be there, unless somebody decides to provide a Gulfstream 550."

"Once they know," Mary said, "maybe they'll provide one, whatever it is. I only told them that his mother was a survivor and that she died long ago. They'll be knocked out of their socks when they hear the news."

Chapter 19

Paul and Heidi had planned to drive interstates 90 and 80 east, that first day, as far as Youngstown, Ohio, and then on Thursday follow 80 to New York, the Tappan Zee Bridge and 95 north to Boston. The blowing snow and increasingly poor visibility changed their plans very quickly. They were more than happy to find Motel 6 lodging off the Ohio Turnpike just southwest of Cleveland. It was after 5 PM before they settled in.

"Two-hundred-and-forty miles in almost eight hours," said Paul. "About thirty miles an hour. Good grief."

"Hot shower and free breakfast," said Heidi. "Count our blessings."

She put her overnight bag on the floor, knelt, and came up with a bottle of California Chardonnay. "Celebrate good times, Pauley. We're alive and together. And now that you've dragged me across state lines, go brush your teeth and I'll turn on the Weather Channel. And charge our phones."

She peered out the window. A world of white. Nothing was moving but swirling sheets of snow. Even El Baba's National Civilian Security thugs were snowbound somewhere. "We just may have to spend the rest of our married life here in North Ridgefield. I'll check for Realtors in the phone book. An Ohio igloo for two."

Dinner was bologna sandwiches, a can of mixed nuts, and the Mondavi. Later, they lay together and listened to the snow sweeping against the window.

"The simple things in life, right, Reverend?"

"Reverend? You promised you wouldn't …"

"Sorry, Paul. I was hoping you'd hear my confession."

"I know what your sins are."

"I'm worried about Father Donahue."

"If that's a sin, I'm guilty too, sweetheart. He put a lot on the line to marry us. Father Neilson knew the circumstances, so, pastor or not, his head could roll as well. That's a Holy Cross Congregation church and very little goes on that doesn't filter back to campus. For both their sakes, I sure hope that doesn't."

"We pretty much ran roughshod over everything, didn't we, Paul? No pre-Cana stuff, no waiting period, no permission from the Bishop …"

"I seem to remember that last one also being violated, rather recently, at an ND commencement ceremony."

"Anyway," said Heidi, "We still have this." She reached over to the bedside table and picked up a white booklet entitled *Together for Life* and waved it in the air.

"Yes," said Paul, "and you still have me and I have you. We owe Father D. and Father Neilson. Now lights out. It will probably take us an hour just to de-ice in the morning."

By 9 AM they were back on the interstate, chatting to one another on their cell phones and snacking on soggy sticky buns and warm coffee from the motel breakfast room. The snow had let up in the night but traffic was at a crawl. They soon found themselves in a long line of cars that was limping along behind a huge yellow truck with a second angled plow that allowed it to clear two lanes at once. *Right now, I'd gladly settle for thirty miles an hour* thought Paul.

He grabbed his cell and called Heidi. Two cars ahead, she picked up.

"Listen, Mrs. Doucette, I'm thinking we might want to get off somewhere just after we cross the state line. Maybe have lunch, gas up, and wait a bit for the roads to get cleared."

"You're the boss. Just tell me when and where."

Paul finally succeeded in edging past the florist's van that had intruded itself between his Expedition and Heidi's 4Runner. Now, as they passed from Ohio to Pennsylvania, he and Heidi exited cautiously into the twenty-four-hour rest area. The red-tiled floor was slippery, the dollar-a-cup coffee from a vending machine was full of grounds, and all the maple benches were occupied, but both were happy to be off the highway. Paul flexed his fingers and rubbed Heidi's shoulders.

"Thank you. That's nice. I was beginning to calcify out there. Clutching that wheel. Maybe we should have waited for the January thaw."

Paul stood checking the wall-size map of Route 80 across Pennsylvania. He glanced outside. "Executive decision. Don't think it's going to get any better in a hurry. Let's get off at Mercer. He pointed. Here—it's only about fourteen miles. Have lunch, find a motel, and spend the night. We're in no rush."

"Sounds good to me, Reverend."

He gave her a hug. "You follow me this time."

On the highway, Paul began to have second thoughts. There seemed to be a lot less traffic and the sky was brightening. *Why stop? Another four days before classes begin at the high school. Might be nice to get back to Gloucester and settle in before the weekend. Give us a chance to relax.* He picked up his cell phone but put it down again, remembering that they both needed to get some gas.

Exit 15 was less than a mile ahead. Paul put on his right turn signal and moved over. Heidi did the same, just as a red pickup truck in the westbound lane on the other side of the median went into a slow skid and began spinning wildly. Paul lost sight of it as he approached the exit ramp and braked slowly.

He glanced in his side view mirror. The red pickup had come to a stop sideways, blocking both westbound lanes. It was directly in the path of a tractor-trailer that had been behind it. The driver of the eighteen-wheeler hit the brakes and his twenty-ton rig responded by jackknifing across the icy median.

"Sweet Jesus, no," said Paul, as he saw the semi sliding across into their lanes. Paul skidded to a stop and reached for the door.

Heidi, who had been watching Paul, looked up to see a massive aluminum wall with TRANS-TERRA in blue lettering dropping from the sky. Her last thoughts were not of Paul, but of the translation "Across the earth."

Chapter 20

There was little doubt in Father Donahue's mind that a virulent storm of gossip was already swirling around the yellow-bricked Main Building. The furtive presence of a junior staffer from ND's office of the provost at Paul and Heidi's wedding had not gone unnoticed by him or Father Neilson, pastor at Christ the King. They both wondered who'd tipped him off.

That meant that news of the marriage of a former confrere of the Holy Cross Congregation to a Morris Inn waitress would likely soon be made known to the Reverend Henry Pankey on his return from California.

Indeed, the university president, California-dreaming and feeling breezy and benevolent, was at that very moment touching down at SBN airport after two weeks in Malibu with his family. It was mid-afternoon and the university's Lear Jet 40XR that had spirited him from Los Angeles was met by a black Lexus driven by a campus security police officer. Father Fischer, Father Pankey's luggage in hand, escorted him to the car, wondering just how he might introduce the topic of the nefarious New Year's Eve nuptials. This would not be a satisfactory reunion with his boss.

By the time they arrived at Sacred Heart, the Reverend Pankey's benevolent demeanor had turned to ice as thick as that on the basilica's parking lot. Father Fischer could feel a migraine coming on as he listened to his instructions.

"This is not a good time for this sort of thing. Not a good time. I have to speak at Sunday's January commencement as you know. Get in touch with Dr. Chambers and Tysheeka. And Father Lewis. They should all be back by now. We'll meet Monday morning. Charlie Donahue has greatly overstepped himself. With us and with the Church. Well, I've dealt with rogue priests before."

Dr. Chambers was chief of staff, Father Lewis counselor to the president and Tysheeka Apollo was special assistant for social justice whose presence was requisite to any meeting that might involve corrective action. *Against man or beast,* thought Father Fischer. *Against student or priest.*

What about Father Donahue? He had great respect for the man but, regrettably, his own first allegiance was to the university and his personal gofer relationship with its president. No point in stirring up the pot. Father Pankey would decide when to call him in. Still, Father Fischer felt extremely discomfited.

It was close to 5 and the "rogue" priest Father Donahue was enjoying a light-hearted conversation with Father Jake Maloney, Stonehill's president. Despite the difference in their ages—Father Jake was only in his 50s—the two had much in common. For more than a month now, they'd been dreaming up a betting pool for the ND-Stonehill game on November 3. Computing the odds was proving to be a major impediment.

They'd also spent some time discussing Paul Doucette, their mutual friend and former philosophy prof at Stonehill. Father Donahue let it be known that he'd joined Paul and Heidi in holy matrimony a few days ago.

"Well, that will no doubt stir up a few waves in your St. Joe River, Charlie. And Paul can probably expect a membership application from the Rent-a-Priest guys. But I know his frustration. He tried valiantly. I'm personally not aware of a single marriage dispensation that was granted by the Vatican in twenty-six years under Paul Two. And their track record hasn't improved under Benedict. The Vatican Ear, you might say, turns a blind eye to almost all such requests. As well as to other annoyances."

"Do you hear that beeping?" asked Father Donahue. "It's happened before. They need to check out these phones."

"Could be call waiting."

"Could be."

"Charlie, it means you have another incoming call. So hit your flash button."

Father Donahue did as instructed. Someone was on the line.

"This is Father Donahue."

"Yes, Brother James Rhodes here. From the congregation's Bishop LaLonde High School in Youngstown. We've met, Father Donahue."

"Of course, how have you been, Brother?"

"Father, this is an emergency call. Right now I'm in Grove City, Pennsylvania. I'm sorry to be the one to tell you, but your friend Paul Doucette and his travelling companion have been in a horrible auto accident not far from here. I regret to say that she lost her life. It was instantaneous. Her car was crushed by an eighteen-wheeler that spun out on the snow. Crossed over the median. A second car hit the truck after it hit her and a man was killed. Paul was in a car ahead of her. He suffered a concussion in a fall from the highway. Took a bad spill running back to what was left of her car. The truck knocked it down an embankment. He asked a state trooper to contact me and I arrived only a short time ago. Route 80 eastbound is paralyzed. I had to come the back roads. Paul gave me your name to call."

Father Donahue put his hand over his face, squeezed his temples, and rubbed his eyes. *May God have mercy on her soul and may His perpetual light shine upon her. Four days they had together. Four days. After ten years of waiting. Shattered dreams.*

"Will Paul be all right?"

"Yes, his body will. His mind is something else. I've never seen anyone so distraught. He's here. Grove City Medical Center. About sixty miles north of Pittsburgh … Father Donahue …?"

"Forgive me, Brother. This is a terrible, terrible shock. Can I talk to him?"

"He's really not lucid, Father. He's been heavily sedated. In great distress and speaking incoherently. Talked about his wife. I didn't know he'd left the order. Was she his wife then?"

"Yes, I married them last Saturday here in South Bend. Very close friends of mine. I'll be there as soon as I can get a flight to Pittsburgh. I'll have to go through Chicago."

"I'll spend the night here, Father, and do what I can for him. The state police are bringing his car here. Can you contact his relatives? And hers?"

"I will. Where did they take her?"

"A local funeral home. I don't know the name yet."

"God bless you, Brother. Expect me tomorrow. I'll call the hospital when I know what time. This is tragic. Calamitous."

Father Donahue knelt by his desk and prayed to the Blessed Mother. For the soul of Heidi Symonds Doucette who was taken at what was probably the happiest time of her life—and for Paul Doucette to find the inner strength to overcome the deep despair that must now engulf him.

By the time he prayed again at his bedside several hours later, he'd booked a one-way flight to Pittsburgh and arranged for his friend at Christ the King, Father David Neilson, to drive him to O'Hare in the morning. He'd given the bad news and the hospital number to Paul's older brother in Massachusetts and asked him to get in touch with Heidi's sister in Dedham.

In his office at Stonehill's Donahue Hall, Father Maloney waited patiently. *He probably just doesn't know how to reconnect,* he thought. He finally put his phone down and turned out the lights.

At the Grove City Medical Center, Brother James Rhodes sat quietly for a long time in the visitor's lounge, watching the snow swirling around the parking lot light stanchions. He wondered when he'd be able to get back to Youngstown and what the repercussions would be from this tragedy—and his role in it. The staff had been kind enough to provide him with a room at the hospital for tonight. It was nearly midnight and he decided to check one more time on Paul Doucette. In the morning he'd let a couple of his other clerical friends in South Bend know what was happening.

Chapter 21

It was the Feast of the Epiphany and Shelby and I were settling in at my place for a 7 PM viewing of the Cotton Bowl from Cowboys Stadium. It mattered not that our Fighting Irish 2011 season had come to a whimpering windup with a Thanksgiving weekend wipeout at Stanford. Their abysmal 3-9 record would go down as the one of the worst in school history.

But we both loved football and were content to watch any BCS matchups. As for the faltering Irish, like our pal Gerry Finn, a Chicago Cubs fan of more than ninety years, ND hopes continued to spring eternal.

Shelby's bird-watching awaited warmer weather. In the meantime, she was experimenting with recipes from a book *(Tidewater on the Half-Shell)* that her mother had sent. Tonight's entrée was to be Smithfield ham and crab. Apparently, Smithfield ham was not available here in northern Indiana, nor were crabs. So it would be HoneyBaked Ham and vegan soy protein. Anything beyond cheese and peanut butter cuisine worked for me.

Shelby put down her wooden spoon and dish to answer the phone. "Mike Meaney," she said, handing it to me.

"Josh, any idea where Father Donahue might be? He appears to have gone AWOL."

"We haven't seen him since Paul and Heidi left Wednesday morning. Is there a problem?"

"Not really. He was supposed to meet me for lunch today and never showed. I can't track him down. Not like him."

"Well, we'll let you know if he turns up, Mike. Right now Shelby's fixing me a Southern specialty and we're watching the Cotton Bowl. Call us if you hear anything." I hung up.

Shelby waved her spoon at me. "And…?"

"Father Donahue's gone missing," I said. "Probably holed up watching the game somewhere."

"Hope he's okay. I've been feeling antsy all day."

"Antsy?"

"You know, like something's going on that we don't know about."

"Like somewhere there's a game of Epiphany poker?"

"Okay, what's that?"

"Seven card draw, but you need Three Kings to open."

Shelby laughed. "You should be ashamed of yourself."

"Well, it's timely."

"Fifteen minutes to dinner. You sit there and watch the cheerleaders. I'm going to give Heidi a call on her cell phone. She told me to keep in touch and they must be there by now. It's been three days."

"Good grief, Shelby, let them get settled in."

Shelby punched in the number. "I just have this urge to call her and say hello."

On Wilson Avenue in Mercer, Pennsylvania, the twisted, snow-covered mass of crushed metal that was once Heidi's 2001 brown 4Runner sat in a corner of the Mercer Auto Salvage yard. No one was nearby to hear the tinny but brave ringtone of "The Notre Dame Victory March" emanating from her cell phone, jammed under what remained of the front seat.

"No answer, Josh. Do you have Paul's number?"

"I don't, Shelby, and I really think it's a bad idea. It's almost nine o'clock back there anyway. Give them a few days and call next week."

Shelby stuck out her tongue at him. "Who appointed you commander-in-cheese?" She tapped his head with her wooden spoon.

In Holy Cross Village, Mike Meaney was getting alarmed. What if Father Donahue had suffered a heart attack jogging around the lake? Winter weather rarely kept the seventy-nine-year old from his exercise regimen. Mike had learned nothing from calls to some of Father

Donahue's clerical friends on campus and even less from several of his associates on the Campus Life Council. Increasingly anxious, he called Father Neilson, pastor at Christ the King.

"Mike, yes, I drove him to O'Hare early this morning. He didn't say where he was going and I didn't ask. So I mentioned it to no one when I got back. We didn't talk much. Not even about the wedding. He was very quiet and I didn't push. Could be a family thing. Just don't know. Whatever it is, it was sudden because he called me late last night."

"And he said nothing about when he was returning?"

"Nary a word. I offered to pick him up but he said he wasn't sure about when that would be. If I had to guess, though, I'd say that he'd received some pretty bad news."

"Well, thank you, Father. I guess we can only wait to hear."

That's that. But odd, thought Mike. *I don't know anything about his family. Or even if he has one.*

Chapter 22

Father Fred Fischer had not expected to be summoned late on a Saturday evening, but now he stood expectantly in the Reverend Pankey's *sanctum sanctorum*, awaiting his orders.

"Father Fischer. Our Monday morning meeting. It's off. The Lord, it seems, has dealt with it in His own way. A tragedy, but one that averts what could have been a major scandal and now clears the road ahead for us. Well, an unfortunate choice of words, perhaps. The bride—of late a waitress on campus—expired in an automobile accident somewhere in Pennsylvania on Thursday. Our runaway playboy Paul Doucette survived and no doubt the community has seen the last of him.

"But it's also clear that Father David Neilson was a willing accomplice in this disgrace and is no longer able, if he ever was, to embrace his pastoral responsibilities at Christ the King. That needs to be repaired. This entire affair is not going to enhance the university's reputation among our friends. But it could have been much worse."

Father Fischer sat stunned. "You're saying Paul's wife was killed?"

"Paul's wife she was not, Father Fischer. Need I remind you of canon law and what a laicized priest can and cannot do? You lie down with dogs and you get up with fleas. Remember that.

"Fortunately, I learned of this before the situation deteriorated. You also should have been aware before now, but, admittedly, this was not a normal occurrence. When Father Donahue returns from Pennsylvania—I've no idea what good he thinks he can do there—we will put it all aside. There is no need to involve Fort Wayne or

Indianapolis, or anyone in this state. Or any other. Have you already spoken with Dr. Chambers, Father Lewis, and Tysheeka?"

"I left messages for them to call me. They all return tomorrow."

"Well, no need to perpetuate it. A misunderstanding. Just apologize for bothering them."

Father Fischer left the office and wondered again why the president of this acclaimed university, holding numerous degrees, including a doctorate from Oxford, and the recipient of many academic and cultural awards, had ever chosen him to be his untitled underling. Had he thought that he might perhaps be somehow related to Fred Fisher, a former trustee and major supporter of Notre Dame? While the late Fred and Sally Fisher had no children, and their surname was spelled differently, anything was possible.

He wandered the snow-covered sidewalks for a while. The doors to the basilica were locked. A half-century ago, he'd been told, before it became a basilica, it was safe haven for undergrads returning from an illicit night out in the Bend. They maybe "got lucky" (heavy hugs and kisses) at Kewpee's hamburger joint with some townie tootsie, or missed the last bus from the stop in front of Joer's.

The night was cold and clear, the students had not yet returned, and the spired skyline of the campus was scarcely visible. He sat on a bench by St. Mary's Lake and lifted his eyes. The moon was waxing gibbous, near full. Its monthly celestial cycles, and those of the stars and planets, were as familiar to him as his fingers and toes.

The interplay between earth and other "heavenly" bodies was like the harmonics between the sections of an orchestra ensemble. It had always fascinated him. He thought on it. A year from tonight and all the calculations of the Maya would be in full flow. *But leave it to the media to hang the names "Doomsday" and "Apocalypse" on what is no more than a unique astronomical event: the alignment of our December solstice sun with the equator of our Milky Way galaxy.*

Right now, Father Fischer found the behavior of Father Pankey far more troubling than the dire predictions of those who saw the galactic alignment of 12-21-12 as the beginning of an ominous "New World" transformation.

Surely the sudden and devastating death of any human being calls for some sympathy and compassion toward those left behind. He had seen none of that tonight from the man who sat in the seat of Sorin. He wondered if Paul Doucette had given his wife the last rites. Despite the dressing down he received from Father Pankey, Father Fischer was familiar enough with canon law to know that an ordained priest always remains a priest and could absolve the sins of the dying.

Even worse, Father Pankey's comments about averting "a major scandal" were duplicitous and pharisaical to say the least. A scandal? A scandal is bestowing a Doctor of Laws on the nation's most zealous pro-abortionist while defying the best advice of the Vatican, the Diocese, dozens of Bishops, and thousands of Catholic luminaries. As Father Pankey had indeed done. *Openly turning his back on the Church.*

While Father Fischer had never expressed his opposition to the honoring of President Mubaraq El Baba on campus, he'd always worried that his position in the Main Building would give the impression that he approved. He did not. He certainly did not. The university had clearly been acting in defiance of Catholic moral principles.

Now, sitting there on a frigid Saturday midnight under a sparkling canopy of stars, when the veil between heaven and earth was at its thinnest, the truth came at him like a blazing ball of fire. It was time to take sides. In his days as a seminarian and long before, he had dreamed of serving as a priest at Notre Dame. But this Notre Dame was not that Notre Dame.

Thanks to Father Pankey, some eighty-eight pro-lifers still faced possible jail time for praying on campus during the El Baba appearance—and our university helps promote the homosexual movement? And strategizes how to "punish" a seventy-nine-year old priest for performing a marriage ceremony? Something very wrong here. Moral values being tossed out the window.

His mind was made up. He'd visit Father Donahue as soon as he returned to campus. He would offer his services. If it meant being a double agent under the Dome, so be it.

He thought of Ephesians 5:11: "Have no fellowship with the unfruitful works of darkness, but rather reprove them."

Chapter 23

It was mid-January and students were reappearing on campus after the holidays. Shelby and I were still in a state of shock following the news of Heidi's death and the subsequent exodus of Father Donahue, who had returned only to pick up his few worldly belongings, thence journey to Stonehill at the invitation of its president, Jake Maloney.

We wondered if ND's leader, the Reverend Pankey, had even been informed. Or had Father Donahue, who had labored in the Holy Cross vineyards quietly and without fanfare these many years, simply chosen to ignore the chain of command. We had yet to contact Paul Doucette, now somewhere back east but, we were told, no longer teaching at Gloucester High School. Anyway, what words could we possibly find to express our feelings? It weighed heavily on us all.

We were also briefly puzzled by several after-hours visits from Father Fred Fischer, Pankey's factotum, who had questioned me earlier about the phone call from our friend Mary Jamieson, "the piper's daughter."

Father Fischer behaved like a man who needed a friend. "I'm so very, very sorry about that accident in Pennsylvania," he told us. "And I'm ashamed of the failure of our administration to respond as they should have. There seems to be a diminishing spirit of true Christianity here. It's really not at all what I'd anticipated."

I was almost embarrassed. The man was not the same man who'd quizzed me before like I was a peeping Tom.

It was on his third visit that he shared a bit of information that added to our depression, yet lifted our spirits somewhat.

"Father Pankey is still annoyed about your friend Mrs. Jamieson. I don't know why. But I wanted to tell you, in confidence if you will, that he had Joe Gallagher send him a copy of your employee performance records."

I was stunned. "What? Why in the world would he do that? Gallagher—and Hesse— never said a word to me."

"They were told not to. He's still got it in his mind that you're interfering in alumni office affairs. That event in autumn, I guess."

"Well, I appreciate you telling me, Father Fischer."

"I was going to mention it to Father Donahue when he returned, but he was here and gone before I knew it."

"You're going out on a limb."

"I understand. But I don't like what's been going on lately and I feel an obligation to help set things right. My family back in Michigan has some idea that I'm second in command here. I can't convince them I'm just a valet slash messenger boy. That doesn't bother me. What does bother me is this continuing series of events that are contra-Catholic. I don't get it."

Shelby looked like she wanted to throw her arms around Father Fischer.

"I hope you will both keep all this in your strictest confidence," he said as he stood up. "And be careful to avoid getting yourselves too involved in the Finn event. Or at least being seen as involved in it. I'm afraid Father Pankey is not a forgiving sort. I'm not nearly as concerned about my own skin as I am about what people are beginning to think about the university."

"We're in your debt, Father."

"No need for that. Just be careful. I'll let you know if there are any more surprises. I've pretty much decided that I should be doing what I think is right. Not what I'm told to do."

He grinned. The first time I'd seen him smile. He looked like a young altar boy. "Never thought I'd be a revolutionary."

After he left, Shelby made us a cup of tea. "What now, wizard?"

"Who knows? This is craziness. Pankey has my employee records? He's getting paranoid. This place is more like DC every day."

"Was Father Fischer putting us on?"

"Not at all. Why would he? Seemed sincere enough. I'd say we now have our own personal fox in the administration's henhouse. Time will tell. I admire the guy for it. Just hope they don't catch on to him."

"Aren't you worried about your job?"

"More than you can imagine, Shelby. We've got to really move out now on Gerry."

Move out we did. Line by line, over the next two weeks, we filled in the many empty blanks of the outline we'd prepared to introduce Gerry to the world. We confirmed our release date: March 22, the date that Harland and Wolff in Belfast began construction on the ship in 1909.

Jack Graney at the *South Bend Sentinel,* who, arms waving, had literally danced around his office when we shared our secret and produced our evidence, was a man given a new purpose in life. His managing editor was equally enthused. "Go for it," he told Jack. They'd set aside a small room for Shelby and me to occupy after hours. A team of three would prepare the mechanics for an international shotgun release that leaned heavily on Internet and worldwide newswires. Another small crew including several part-timers and interns would deal with e-mail, snail mail and telephone queries.

The big city state-controlled dailies, at least those still feigning impartiality, were farther down our distribution list. I'd given Jack and his team guarded copies of all the documents and photos we had: Gerry's birth certificate from November 3, 1912, his mother's *Titanic Survivor's Certificate of Death* from 1968, and, of course, the telling Somerset County photo of young Gerry and his mother with her rescuer, Mary Jamieson's dad, the *Titanic* piper. We called Mary and told her she'd be hearing from Jack's *Titanic* Team. They visited her the following weekend and did several video interviews.

"Nice boys," she told us. "And they took me out to lunch!"

Two domain names had been purchased (www.survivor1912.org and www.titanic100th.org). The sites were under construction and would be hosted on the *Sentinel*'s server.

There were thousands of *Titanic*-related Web sites on our e-mail list that touched on *Titanic* art, books, films, music, cults, history, and every conceivable aspect of the tragedy. In fact, an Internet search of the name *Titanic* spat out over a million choices.

Two of the *Sentinel*'s reporters, a photographer, and I set up a visit with Gerry Finn. We knew it was just a question of time before our secret would be leaked. But we kept our fingers crossed. This would be news that even the head-in-the-sand, lame-stream media would have to acknowledge.

It was a peculiar time to take a vacation but we'd requested a week off. Hesse, uncharacteristically, had obliged without a complaint.

Sports were sluggish but the fortunes of the ND basketball team had improved to where it looked like they might, after all, make it at least to the NIT openers on March 21, the day before our announcement. I hadn't even considered that. My official specialty was football, but I was a "secondary" on hoops and baseball—and a "backup" on all of the university's twenty-one other sports.

Our high-tech communications set-up in the office let us view all the basketball road games on a Samsung high-def screen that was taller than our team's 6'11" center. Every play was on tape for us to review. On a normal evening, our game recaps and stats were completed and released just minutes after the end of the game.

It was a long way, I thought, from the old "Grid Graph" of the 1920s that Gerry Finn had told me about. To view an "away" football game, someone who was also hooked into a Western Union telegraph would move a flashlight behind a huge pane of glass (often in the shape of a pigskin) to show the progress of the ball to a standing audience. Later improvements showed lights representing the name of each player, the game clock, score, etc. In downtown South Bend, during the '20s, a Grid Graph was erected above the outside entrance to one of the student's favorite hangouts.

In any case, at the moment I was more interested in the Gerry Finn project than my job. Father Fischer had told us that Father Charlie Donahue was now back at Stonehill and was an assistant professor of history, as well as athletic chaplain. Father Donahue had been happy to pack his bags and return to the 'Hill at the invitation of Father Maloney. He'd had a bellyful of the "new" Notre Dame and its progressive pomposity.

Father David Neilson remained as pastor of Christ the King. No one seemed to know where Paul Doucette had gone after Heidi's burial in Calvary Cemetery in Gloucester. Shelby and I grieved for them both, two animated and happy people who had come into our lives and were gone just as quickly.

Our visit to Gerry went off without a hitch. He was high-spirited and clearly looking forward to it all. Photos were taken of him wearing his Cubs uniform, holding up the brass button from the piper's overcoat, displaying the memorial *Sinking of the Titanic* book and holding up his birth certificate. The guys from the *Sentinel* did two video interviews with him sitting in front of the "Grand Staircase" at the *Titanic* exhibition in the Chicago Museum of Science & Industry. He was at the top of his game. (*"The secret to longevity? Don't fall down and don't stop breathing."*) After five hours with Gerry and his daughter Dorothy, they came back as believers. It was going to be hard to keep them silent.

We were scheduled to return to work on Monday, February 6, and we felt considerably better about "The Finn Phenomenon." But it remained a mammoth undertaking and we had numerous info lines set in place at the *Sentinel* to take queries as well as "hot lines" to pick up calls to Gerry's home phone. After March 22, the *South Bend Sentinel* would be a very well-known newspaper.

Chapter 24

Students entering the campus dining halls for the evening meal that Sunday night were greeted by the usual card-check brigade of elderly South Bend ladies. They were wearing kelly-green *hijab* underscarves and handing out small white lapel buttons picturing a dinner plate flanked by knife and fork and, in Farsi, the words "Eat halal."

What was the occasion? Unknown to most, but soon to be known to many, was that February 5, 2012, was *Mawlid-al-Nabi*, the birthday of Mohammad. The best was yet to come for those not yet in the line of daily specials, usually the most popular of serving stations. Awaiting their jaded American palates was the day's offering of Persian *halal* lamb patties, steamed rice, grated apples, and flat *naan* bread.

The reaction of hungry students to the one and one-quarter-inch "Eat halal" lapel buttons and the chow hall trays full of Persian *halal* lamb patties was immediate and predictable.

It took only mere minutes. First, several buttons were put to the Ultimate Frisbee test, and then more, and many more, until the air was filled with skimming "Eat halal" discs. Geraldine Kretzemeyer, a freshman from Akron, was one of the first casualties. The metal pin-back intended to clasp the button to one's clothing pinned itself to Geraldine's left ear. Blood flowed freely. First and worst campus casualty of the night's Muslim melee.

Somewhat generously defined according to *Sharia*, the harsh and radical Islamic laws, *halal* means any object or action permissible to eat, engage in, or otherwise use. As the buttons bounced sharply off walls, tables, heads, and torsos, the *halal* lamb patties and *naan* bread were launched with more satisfying and less dangerous results. Those not "engaged in" this *halal* fled the scene or sought to hide under the tables.

One day back in the mid-50s when ND students were given a reduced ration of milk, the subsequent flurry of glasses to the tiled floor was eventually made known to the *South Bend Sentinel* and thence to the *Chicago Tribune*. Now, almost sixty years later, while Persian lamb patties and buttons were still airborne, cell phone photos were instantaneously arriving in homes and even some newsrooms the nation over. Even close-ups of Geraldine Kretzemeyer's bloody ear and chow hall card-checker Mrs. Julia Laskowski with her gray hair tumbling Arab-illegally out of her *hijab* were already circulating on Facebook.

As someone later commented, it was one *halal* of a night and would be recalled by many as the Mohammad Birthday Massacre. Yet another case of very bad judgment by the college's administration. Word was that they had been strongly encouraged by someone (who knew who?) to provide "a memorable student observance of Muslim tradition." As indeed it was.

Shelby and I knew none of this as we labored that Sunday evening at my apartment, listing more and more outlets and targets for the March 22 announcement.

Sunday's chow hall fracas was a lead story on Monday AM radio. I heard about it driving to campus. The administration, in its usual one-step, two-step evasion of events, offered a terse response to media queries. "We deplore the racist actions of a few misguided students and they will be dealt with. Our deepest apologies to our Muslim students and their families." The university's food services, in understandable lockstep, was as close-mouthed as a Cherrystone Clam. It was embarrassing.

I'd been away for just a week but sensed an undercurrent of change in the office when I appeared Monday morning. Shelby was not yet there. I wondered why my dozen or so co-workers greeted me with some obvious apprehension. I found out quickly. Father Donahue had been oh so right.

Even before I'd hung up my coat, Hesse was there. He normally arrived after 9 AM. He invited me into his office and closed the door.

"Sit down, Josh. I'll get to the point.

"Not good news. Not good at all. And I'm sorry. Joe Gallagher called me at home last night and said we're overrunning our budget big-time. Not necessarily our part of communications but the whole shebang. The bottom line is he's making some painful cuts across the board and we're going to have to let you go. It's a helluva time to tell you this, starting the new year and all. I'm truly sorry."

"You're kidding me."

"You'll get three months' severance pay and full pay for any unused vacation. I told Joe you needed only three months to get your ten in and qualify for pension, but he said we couldn't make exceptions to policy. You might want to talk to him about that or make an appeal to someone over in the Main Building."

Gallagher was the top dog in the university's multi-pen public information kennel. Other than departmental Christmas parties, my contact with him had been next to nil. I couldn't even remember the last time he'd visited our office. I copied him on every "Chalk Talk" column I did for the *Sentinel,* but doubted he even read them.

"I also told him you were probably our best writer and certainly our best man to work that Stonehill game." Hesse was busy trying to calm the waves as I struggled to filter the news about my pension.

"Joe is usually pretty accommodating, but it's like he wasn't even listening. Maybe if you go chat with him. You might turn it around. I'm sorry, Josh. I did my best."

I was spitting mad, but finally recovered myself. "Don, what the hell is going on? Why me? I'm not the most expensive guy on the payroll by a long shot. There has to be more to this than just cost cutting. What's behind it? I know you sent my records over to Hankey Pankey. What the hell is this all about?"

"Josh, I really don't know. I'll tell you honestly. This pisses me off no end. You're my top performer and I told Joe. For whatever reason, he's dug in. Not like him."

I felt like I'd taken a blind-side body blow from some three-hundred-pound lineman. This couldn't be happening. *You can't do this to me,* I thought. *I know this place, I know the game, I know the team. And I know Stonehill, their teachers, their players. Somebody help me.*

Hesse went on babbling about job assistance and insurance while I tried to collect myself. I'd have to walk out of here with Shelby and the others watching. She didn't know, but I bet some of the others did.

So a memorable February 6 it was. The birthday of ND's founder Father Edward Sorin. And, one of the few dates I remembered from my high school American history class on Cape Cod. The day that Massachusetts became a state. February 6, 1788. Maybe I should have just stayed up there.

Chapter 25

Up there, at Stonehill College in North Easton, there were not many among the faculty who remembered Paul Doucette, the Holy Cross priest and former philosophy professor. Even though he had left the college only a dozen years ago. But when word of his separation from the priesthood, his marriage, and his bride's tragic death began circulating, memories were jogged. "One of the really good guys," it was agreed.

Now, a month after the accident, Doucette was still not to be found. His cell phone had apparently been disconnected and his home in Gloucester was on the market.

Stonehill President Father Jake Maloney had been discussing Doucette with Father Donahue at the very moment the news of Heidi's death was reaching South Bend. Later, when Maloney learned that Notre Dame's trustees were about to pitch Donahue overboard, he'd been more than happy to throw a life preserver his way. Now they both worried over Doucette.

"I'd be delighted to see him back here," said Maloney. "We both know other clergy who called it quits."

"You have a couple here at the Hill," said Father Donahue, "and there are a half dozen or so at Notre Dame, including a pair of ex-Jebbies. Runaways from Marquette and St. Louis U. But you'd be fortunate to get Paul."

"Well, we're glad to have you back, Charlie. The place has changed a bit since your day, I'm sure. We have some grads not entirely happy."

He could have been talking about Lou Gasparini, Class of '52. Lou was never a student of Father Donahue but had been a friend and now he had high hopes that Donahue would set a few things right.

At that very moment, Lou was holding forth fiercely to a pair of pals in a corner booth of the Lazy River Café, a local sixty-year-old sports pub. The walls were adorned with a century's worth of fishing paraphernalia. Mounted bass, perch, and walleye. Glass-fronted boxes cluttered with well-worn, colorful lures from another era. Wooden bobbers, sinkers, and boxes of hooks from L.L. Bean, sandwiched between rusty outboard motors. Directly above Lou, a sixteen-foot skiff with oars, tackle boxes rods, reels, and creels, all threatening to come down on him at any moment.

Lou was also having another of his GERD altercations. *Damn coffee did it every time. Or just plain stress.*

And stressed was how he felt. He wasn't at all pleased with his alma mater. And he knew he wasn't alone. The more he saw, the less he liked. Liberalism running riot. The Hill wasn't the place it had been in his day. Caving to this Ivy League look-alike posturing.

He waggled a finger at two of his old classmates. "Maybe Father Donahue will get the college back in the fold. It's a lost sheep. Remember how innocent it was back then? A Catholic college, under Catholic control, and a Catholic curriculum. Now? Now it's a 'selective' Catholic college. Whatever the hell that means. Getting awards from El Baba's 'Community Service' programs. All under something called 'United We Serve.' Huh. Read AmeriCorps, ACORN, and Lord knows what else for that! Feely good stuff for the masses. Money, lots of it, for El Baba boosters and voters. How long before he shows up to talk to *our* graduates?"

"That'll never happen," said Larry Barry. "I think you're going overboard on all this. Do you have a toothache or something?"

"Don't be too sure," said Lou. "We're headed in the same direction as Notre Dame, and that ain't good. Seems like we started compromising a lot of things back there in the early '70s. Right after our Holy Crossers declared their independence from the Catholic Church.

"Did you know we have organizations on campus to update you about your sexual orientation? In case you weren't sure. And do you guys remember anybody ever telling us that we were not to apply whipped cream or paint to someone else's body? Or that we weren't allowed to kidnap another student and place him or her in bondage?"

They both laughed. "Come on, Lou," said Larry. "Didn't the administration dump those boxes of condoms that some nitwits put around the dorms a few years ago? You're babbling."

"Think so? Check out the Hill Book. Some of the Do's and Don't's for today's student population."

"Times change, Lou," said Ed Wright, another '52 grad.

"You aren't kidding, pal. We were founded by the congregation, they're quick to say that, but they're not in charge these days. I think we got caught up in that same Land O'Lakes buttery crap. Three times more lay trustees than priests, not a few of them thick as bread dough with those robber barons in Washington.

"Any of you looked at what they're studying these days? Studying, my foot. More of that warm, touchy, fuzzy stuff. Handing out degrees for 'Gender Studies.' Encouraging everybody to 'find themselves.'"

Barry bristled. "Who have you been talking to? My granddaughter Patsy loves the place. And she's one smart kid."

"What's her major?"

"Theatre arts."

"What is it? What can she do with it?"

"I don't know. But she's happy. She's spending next semester in France. Then get her BM in Music/Theatre. Don't ask."

"You've made my point. These days it's one big holiday. Cell phones, college credit cards, trips abroad, *kumbaya* conventions. When do they actually study? I wouldn't have minded spending a semester guzzling Guinness in Limerick or a year quaffing Doppelbock in Heidelberg."

Barry and Ed Wright looked for their waiter.

"You're foaming at the mouth, Lou," said Wright. "And I've got to get out of here."

"Me too," echoed Barry.

"What's the rush? You guys don't have anywhere to go. Why don't you go over to the college and see who's hooking up with whom? That's the PC term these days for shacking up. Do you know what their policy for so-called overnight guests is? Check it out."

"Check it out? Maybe he's getting gout," said Ed as they exited the Lazy River Café.

Chapter 26

Mike Meaney met me at my apartment door as I was carrying in a brown cardboard box containing the contents of my desk. We went inside and I opened a couple of bottles of Four Horsemen Irish Red Ale. I'd have to think about buying another brand.

"A good Jewish lawyer, that's what you need, Josh. You'd clean up and send a message to those egos in the Main Building."

"I'm past being mad. I don't want to clean up. Three months short or not, I just want to get my pension and get off that campus. There must be some sort of law that says your employer can't require ten years service for a pension and then axe you after nine and three-quarters. It's not like they're hurting for bucks."

"Agree, and technically, the law is on their side. However, you were told that the budget was being overrun and they'd have to make some painful cuts. I still have friends on campus and I checked that out. Both untrue. They lied to you. Also, they're paying you three months severance which implies you're on their payroll for another three months, right?"

"Is Meaney a Jewish name, Mike? You're hired."

"I think you need to go and talk to Joe Gallagher. Your big boss, well, ex-big boss. Let him know you're on to them. Make sure you wear a jacket and stop by here before you go in. I want to add a little something to your inside pocket."

I did exactly that the next morning. I pushed the "Rec" button before I entered Gallagher's office.

He came from behind his desk with hand extended. "I've been expecting you. Don Hesse said you might be over. I'm sorry I haven't made it a point to talk to you sooner."

I touched his hand and sat down.

"Well, it's only been three days. You're busy, but I needed to hear it from you." The words tumbled out. "And I need to tell you a few things, the first of which has to do with my pension. I know the university has an All-American, five-star legal team, but this grievance is not going to go away in a hurry. I had nine years and nine months in that job or exactly ten years if you throw in my three months severance. So if it takes me the rest of my life to turn this around, then so be it. I've talked to a couple of old-timers who cut their teeth on the law here. They're interested. Very interested.

"And it's also obvious to everyone in our department that the business about a budget overrun is a red herring. I was lied to. I seem to be the only one affected. My friends, unnamed for now, also tell me that I was viewed as next in line to replace Hesse. They'd make good witnesses. I'm not looking for a pat on the back. But let's be honest here. What gives?"

Gallagher leaned back in his chair and steepled his fingers. I could visualize a dump truck with a load of manure backing up in my direction.

"Josh, I hear you. I know very well that much of what you've done has gone unrecognized. Believe me, I'm familiar with who does the work and who gets the credit. In high school, I was walking home one afternoon and heard some kid screaming. He'd fallen through the ice. I scaled a fence and climbed over some slippery rocks. One step and I knew I'd go through myself. I tried to belly it, but no dice. Two cops showed up. One tossed a rope to me. I made a lasso, whirled it over my head a few times in the best Roy Rogers style, and let fly. God was at my side. That rope landed right over the kid's head and eventually I dragged him across the ice to the fence. When I got home, my mom and dad asked me if I'd been in a fight. I told them what happened. Next week the local paper ran a picture of both cops holding the smiling boy. No mention of me. I learned early."

He yawned and looked like he wanted to end this discussion right now. I wanted to tell him to shut up, write it up, and send it to *Reader's Digest*.

"Joe, why did you give Father Pankey my employee records?"

"He requested them. He's the top rung on the ladder, as you know."

"And what reason did he give for pushing me out?"

"Well, I shouldn't repeat this. He claimed you were interfering with the alumni office. And doing outside work on company time. Reason enough. And when I mentioned your pension? 'Absolutely not,' he said. 'Ten years is ten years. Not nine point seven-five.'

"Hesse and I both told him you were pretty much the up-and-comer on the Sports Info staff, but he was insistent. We had to back off."

"Well, he's made it worse on himself. The *Sentinel* is only waiting my okay to publish a story on how I was duped. Railroaded. And I challenge anyone to show that I did not put in my eight a day—and more—on the job. If he's talking about helping out on Gerry Finn's hundredth, none of that was done on university time."

Joe shrugged. "Don't forget your little trip with Shelby to Missouri."

He was right, but I continued. "This is exactly the kind of story that the media loves. Especially involving ND. You know that. You can tell Father Pankey that his popularity polls are going to take another hit."

"I'm really sorry, Josh. I know it's not exactly fair. But he's the captain of the good ship Notre Dame and we do what we're told."

"I'll be on my way then. But you might mention that his ship is about to hit an iceberg."

I turned off the tape recorder and headed for Mike Meaney's apartment in Holy Cross Village. He did a little cha-cha when he listened to Joe Gallagher quoting Father Pankey calling me a trouble-maker and Joe himself admitting that "it's not fair."

"Ah hah," he said. "And nary a word in defense of budget overruns. We got 'em."

I left the tape with him and he promised to make a couple of copies.

I spent the rest of the day at the *Sentinel*, reviewing the videos of our interviews with Gerry Finn, and doing yet another backgrounder to respond to media questions. The links between Kate Curran Finn, her Uncle Will Curran, the piper Eugene Dolan, and his daughter Mary Dolan Jamieson in Missouri were indisputable and backed up by photos and documents. We had copies of them all on our Web sites and ready to go on e-mail. It was all the proof we needed to support our findings.

The big problem would be one of faith and morals. How many would accept a baby in the womb as a real person? We didn't care. We just wanted the university leaders to do so. They'd be asked. Not to uphold life would even further dilute their claim to be Catholic. Father Pankey would be put to the test once more while everyone watched.

The *Sentinel* reporter assigned to the story of my termination had already requested an interview with Pankey. Predictably, he had been turned down, but he was making calls to others on campus who knew me. I'd given him several phone numbers, including Father Fischer's.

If the week had begun on a very bad note, it was about to end on an exceedingly good one. I picked up a couple of ham sandwiches (Lent didn't begin until next week) and met Shelby Friday noon down by St. Mary's Lake. She was unusually cheerful considering I was now without gainful employment.

"You need some cheering up, Josh. We have a reservation at the LaSalle Grill tomorrow night. Seven o'clock. My treat."

"Shelby …"

She put her hand on my knee. " I have a good feeling about all this. It will work out. The truth, and the real Notre Dame, are on your side. Remember how I said it's like there's always another life, an undercurrent of some kind, an unseen inner circle on this campus? I've felt really tuned in to it this week. Like we're part of it. It's favorable. You're being helped. Do you know what I'm saying?"

"Shelby…"

"Say nothing. And after dinner tomorrow we're going to my place and dance in the dark." Her cat's eyes glistened. My heart soared.

I walked her back to the office and drove down to the *Sentinel*. I was beginning to feel like I was on their payroll. That afternoon Jack Graney asked me if I would like to be. I didn't need a lot of time to think it over. Jack already had one assistant sports editor and I would be a second.

The *Sentinel* would match my previous salary and the university would be my beat. It couldn't have worked out better. "If you're healthy," said Jack, "you can start Monday."

I went home early, wondering if Shelby maybe was in tune with the spirits. It got better. My message minder was blinking. Joe Gallagher wanted to talk. I drove out to the campus and we talked. The university was extending an olive branch. If I would arrange to have the *Sentinel* story of my termination killed, my pension would be safe.

"You also need to destroy any copies of that tape you made on me," he said. I gaped at him.

He grinned. "You'll never make it in the CIA. It was pretty obvious."

"Why didn't you …"

"Hey, I'm in your corner. I knew you were getting screwed, so I decided to give you a little ammo. Anyway, you can thank our lawyers. We'll put it all in writing for you to sign. Come by my place tomorrow. Father Pankey resisted, but not for long. He can be pretty hardnosed at times. Tell me you're not wired now."

I thanked Jack, stopped by his place the next day and signed the waiver.

"You're some kind of mystic," I told Shelby Saturday night. "Stay close to me. Stand by me."

We had a lot to celebrate, and we did. Into the wee hours. It was, after all, almost Valentine's Day.

"You're here in my heart," I sang to her, "and my heart will go on."

Chapter 27

I'd planned to pick up Shelby for the 10:30 at the basilica, but the telephone changed that. It was 4:15 AM and Melanie Moore with the London *Daily Mail* "would like to chat' with me.

I should have known better. Father Donahue had been right when he told us, "Get thee busy. Move your timetable up!" Now I would pay the price for procrastinating.

Melanie didn't mince words. "Josh Allen?"

"Yes?"

"So what are you smoking? You've found a live bod named Gerard Finn who sailed on the Big T? You've got to be joking."

"Miss Moore, it's four in the morning. Give me your number or e-mail address and I'll get back to you." (*But not on my home telephone,* I thought.)

"I've checked the passenger list, Mr. Allen. All the lists. Sorry to wake you. There's no one named Finn on them. Never has been. You've been goosed, as they say. *Titanic* is one of my loves. I've written a dozen stories about her. What's your source?"

I'd grown a thick anti-media skin in a decade. And I knew that the *Daily Mail* made the *National Enquirer* look like the Book of Kells. I asked again. "What's your number? And how did you get mine?"

"I'll need to hear from you within the hour."

"Don't count on it. I'm an independent. And I'm back to bed."

I cut her off, called Shelby, dressed quickly, and headed out.

Melanie's call was a call to arms for all of us. By 9 AM, Shelby, I, and two others of the *Sentinel's "Titanic Team"* were drinking coffee, asking the Lord's forgiveness for missing mass, and ready to make all the appropriate keystrokes that would introduce Gerry Finn to the world.

"How did she find out?" I asked. More to myself than to anyone.

"Beats me," said Shelby. "I checked as soon as you called me at O-Dark-Thirty this morning. *Nada.*"

Sunday morning or not, we agreed quickly to advance our release date by six weeks. Like now. Our Web sites were up and running and we let it go from Titanic1@sbsentinel.com as Shelby sang, "Nearer My God to Thee." What were the rest of the words to that hymn? We called Mary in Missouri and Gerry in Chicago to alert them. They were as excited as kids on their first date. We left messages for Ed Wagner and Father Donahue at Stonehill and I called Bill Curran in Jersey to update him.

It would, of course, be the *Sentinel's* page one lead on Monday. And include all the appropriate sources, photos, and interviews on jump pages.

It was to be the journalistic equivalent of knocking down a bald-faced hornets' nest with one's bare hands.

———————————

Last *Titanic* Survivor Still Alive— ### ND's Gerard Finn, 99, Was There

SOUTH BEND, IN, Feb. 12, 2012...Following a three-month investigation, the *South Bend Sentinel* has verified that 99-year old Gerard Finn of Chicago, a retired accountant and currently the oldest alumnus of the University of Notre Dame, is the last living survivor of the RMS *Titanic* sinking in the North Atlantic. Finn was one of 10 *in utero* children aboard the ship when it collided with an iceberg on April 14, 1912.

The distinction of last living survivor had previously been accorded to England's Millvina Dean who died at age 97 on June 1, 2009, the 98th anniversary of the *Titanic's* launching.

Gerard Finn's mother, Katherine Curran Finn from County Cavan, Ireland, was 23 and in her third month of pregnancy when she boarded *Titanic* at Queenstown, Ireland, on April 11, 1912. She was among the 705 survivors of maritime history's greatest disaster who were rescued by the Cunard Line's *Carpathia*. Gerard, her only child, was born on Nov. 3 that year in Morristown, N.J., and went on to graduate from Notre Dame in 1934. His mother died on July 5, 1948, in New York City.

Mrs. Finn was pulled into a lifeboat by fellow passenger Edward Dolan, whose daughter Mary Dolan Jamieson, 87, is a resident of Unity, Mo., and who is still active in *Titanic*-related historical events. Her father Edward and Gerard Finn's mother Katherine Curran Finn kept in contact after the disaster and were photographed together in 1918 at the Basking Ridge, N.J., home of Mrs. Finn's uncle, William J. Curran. Mrs. Jamieson was able to identify her father in that photo, found recently among Gerard Finn's mementos.

More than 1,500 perished when *Titanic* collided with an iceberg on April 14, 1912. The 100th anniversary of the sinking will be marked this year by a large number of events, including cruises by several ships following the same itinerary as the *Titanic*.

Mrs. Jamieson will be among the guest speakers at several historical society programs planned during the month of April this year.

Mr. Finn will celebrate his 100th birthday on Nov. 3. He will be honored as Notre Dame's first Centenarian Award recipient at ceremonies during the football game that day between the Irish and Stonehill College, Easton MA, also run by the congregation of the Holy Cross.

# # #

Note to Editors:

Photos, Video Interviews, supporting documents, and contacts available at www.survivor1912.org and www.titanic100th.org.

Chapter 28

I was very happy that I had taken the time to visit Joe Gallagher on Saturday afternoon and sign the *quid pro quo* waiver guaranteeing my pension. Joe called me at the *Sentinel* office to say that the university was most definitely not pleased with the early publicity the *Sentinel's* announcement had generated. Soon after, Father Fischer rang my cell phone.

"How's your leader taking it?" I asked.

"He's not giving thanks. Forgive me for saying it, but he's up there going off like a Roman candle." *An apt Catholic clerical analogy*, I thought.

"Quite a few calls coming in," he told us. "They haven't decided how to respond or even if to respond. Right now they're referring all calls to your paper."

We'd hand-delivered a copy of our complete release to ND's Main Building on Sunday morning. It would have been clear to anyone reading it that we hadn't attributed anything to the university.

But the online edition of the once venerable, but now grayer-by-the-day, *New York Times* had, as usual, sought to interpose its anti-religious bias. Father Pankey and the trustees were understandably upset with it.

Irish Mythology
The beleaguered University of Notre Dame, still reeling from criticism by Catholic Church officials for

its commencement speaking invitation to President Mubaraq El Baba, took another awkward step backward yesterday when it claimed that its oldest alumnus, Gerard Finn of Chicago, was the last living survivor of the 1912 *Titanic* disaster.

Finn's mother, who was pregnant when she boarded the ship in Ireland on April 11, 1912, was one of the 705 saved. Her son, now 99, was, understandably, not on the passenger list. (He was born the following November in New Jersey.)

"I don't know what sort of game they're playing. Our Millvina Dean was the last survivor and she died three years ago. Full stop," said Dr. Marshall Clark, secretary of the renowned British Titanic Historical Society. "Even Notre Dame officials must know that a two- or three-month old fetus is merely the product of conception and not a person. What do they hope to gain by this misfire?"

It was futile to point out that the *Times* had badly botched the facts as well as the source. Besides, I was delighted that they had so quickly cut to the issue that we wanted to get on the table. Would Notre Dame defend the rights of the unborn? Would they uphold the sanctity of human life in its embryonic stages?

Most annoying to the administration, of course, was the fact they had been made to look foolish in the one publication that was the darling of the east coast, godless, secular academic society that Notre Dame's trustees desperately sought to join. I wondered how many phone calls and e-mails had already arrived at the Main Building. Father Fischer would no doubt keep us posted.

The story was out there now. Everywhere. It was going to be a long, uphill fight. This was the sort of thing the current generation of "reporters" loved. There were legions of quotable, anti-life, sideline pundits who would delight in attacking the pro-life forces when there was no fear of being challenged. Given the opportunity, the media were like maggots and blowflies descending on an animal's carcass.

The Chicago Tribune, with deep roots in the Midwest Notre Dame community and alums within their hierarchy, was careful not to step on too many hands.

ND Oldest Grad a *Titanic* Survivor?

One-hundred years after the sinking of the RMS *Titanic* with the loss of 1,500 lives, Gerard Finn, a Chicago resident and at 99 the oldest alumnus of the University of Notre Dame, has been identified as a survivor of that "unsinkable" ill-fated White Star Line ship.

Finn was one of 10 *in utero* children aboard *Titanic* when it collided with an iceberg on April 14, 1912. His mother, Kate Curran Finn, was among 705 rescued by the ship RMS *Carpathia*. Her son was born in New Jersey on Nov. 3 that year.

The announcement yesterday by the *South Bend Sentinel* is sure to trigger an ideological tsunami of biblical proportions among maritime historians, theologians, politicians, and even disciples of the 2012 "Doomsday" prophecies.

The *Sentinel* noted that the "oldest living survivor" distinction had previously been accorded Millvina Dean of Southampton, UK, who died at age 97 on June 1, 2009, the 98th anniversary of the *Titanic*'s launching.

Finn will receive ND's first Centenarian Award on his 100th birthday in South Bend at the first football game between the Irish and Stonehill College, Easton, Mass. Stonehill was also founded by the congregation of the Holy Cross.

Elaine Langan with the Illinois Right to Life Federation said the recognition was "a wonderful surprise. The fetus is a young human being and is perfectly formed at three months," she said. "We applaud Notre Dame and the South Bend newspaper for its investigation and story. God bless Gerard Finn."

Nancy Bachmann with Planned Parenthood of
Illinois called the announcement "ridiculous."
(See pages 7-8A for expanded story.)

I knew the Trib treatment would further chafe the ND
administration's raw skin. The right-to-lifers had naturally assumed
the university was supportive of our announcement.

My friend Melanie Moore with the London *Daily Mail* had feasted
on our Sunday release. Her brief online piece was sandwiched between
"School Bans Boys and Girls under 15 from Wearing Skirts" and
"Husband Drives Milk Truck over Jealous Wife."

Finn the Fetus Covets Our Millvina's Crown

American envy knows no bounds. The Yanks have
now chosen to rewrite the darkest day of maritime
history by introducing Gerard Finn, a 99-year old
resident of crime-ridden Chicago, as an aspirant to the
title of "Sole Living Titanic Survivor," held legitimately
by our Millvina "Queen" Dean until her death in
2009. It matters not that Finn, the would-be usurper
of Millvina's throne, wasn't born until seven months
after the ship sank. Stay tuned for further episodes of
the Finn Fantasy Follies.

Melanie's shot across our bows was standard fare for the *Mail*.
There was much worse yet to come, we knew. London's *Daily Telegraph*
acknowledged our release by a passing mention ("The Great Finn
Fraud") in its "Weird" section ("…because news doesn't have to be
serious"). It was clear that any demotion of Millvina Dean would not
be welcome in "England's green and pleasant land."

One Irish tabloid cartoonist had a frightened baby popping his head
out from under his mother's skirt and asking "Does no one else see that
iceberg in front of us?"

Opportunists were ever present that week and occasionally a few
vultures descended. A guy in Saskatchewan wanted us to get Gerry's
handprint on a hunk of clay and send it back to use as a mold. He

promised $3,000 up front and a dollar on every ceramic handprint he sold after that. On the same day, a company that sold a video game called Save the Titanic offered Gerry $2,000 to endorse its product.

Titanic artifact exhibitions were unsure. Some ignored the release. Others contacted us asking for interviews with Gerry or personal items, including clothing.

In Chicago, Gerry's e-mail in-box and postal pigeonhole were overflowing. A smattering of marriage proposals, nastygrams from pro-choicers, threats of lawsuits from some wackos in the UK, and mega invitations to speak. One was from a politician in Australia who claimed his grandfather worked for Harland & Wolff, the Belfast builder of Titanic. He said he'd send his own plane from Sydney to pick up Gerry.

It was going to take a lot of time to sort it all out. There was one, however, we all agreed to within minutes of reading it: an offer from the new Chicago Cubs owner for Gerry to throw out the first pitch at the home opener against Atlanta.

Down in Unity, Mary Dolan Jamieson was beside herself with glee. Two local television stations were parked outside her modest home. Her phone rang constantly. A seventy-five-year-old photo of her with her dad ran on page one of the St. Louis Post's "People" section. And a St. Louis judge and distant relative of Titanic survivor Elisabeth Walton Allen (the first to board the rescue ship Carpathia) offered to fly Mary to Massachusetts to speak at the April 14 gala marking the Titanic centennial.

As expected, the Internet became a battleground for pro-life and pro-choice forces. Our two Web sites took thousands of hits in the first seventy-two hours. Our video interviews and photos of Gerry Finn and Mary Dolan were everywhere on social networking sites. At a time when people were searching for something to replace their animosity and exasperation with a tyrannical government, Gerry became something of an overnight American Idol and was kept busy signing handout photos of himself and talking on his Titanic hotline.

"Is the president aware of Gerry Finn?" a member of the White House press corps asked Raashid Roberts, El Baba's new press secretary. Roberts tugged at his coffee-colored, elfin ear and laughed. "Finn should have been put down long ago. An imposter. It hasn't helped our relationship with Number Ten Downing. I believe the president has apologized to the prime minister. Next?"

It was a hectic week. Despite the surfeit of downloadable information and documents available to the world on our Web sites, we still put in twelve-hour days responding to calls and e-mails.

Our "team" rewarded itself with a dinner out at a Mishawaka steak house the following Saturday night. As luck would have it, our waiter, Gavin, had grown up in the UK.

"Gavin, ever heard of Gerry Finn?"

"Who hasn't?"

"He came over on the Titanic."

Gavin just smiled. "One third of him did, anyway. Ready to order?"

Chapter 29

March came in like the proverbial lion, albeit a wet one, and with it a continuing stream of controversy. The university had yet to make any public pronouncements on Gerry Finn, other than to say, "We consider this a private matter and, as such, we do not comment. At this time, Mr. Finn is scheduled to receive the first Alumni Centenarian Award on November 3."

We could only shake our heads. "A private matter"? And "at this time" *("at this time"!)* he "is scheduled to receive" the award? They were sounding more and more like the Bureau of Bogus Bumblers in the White House.

Come out from under your rock, I thought.

One of the lead editorials in *The Observer,* the student daily newspaper, had been headed "Embryo Imbroglio" and concluded with this:

The *Sentinel's* thesis is one level above a fairy tale and one level below a *National Enquirer* front-pager. It serves no purpose except to further antagonize those on both sides of the Right to Life issue and to stem useful engagement and dialogue. That it should even receive such attention is absurd. Gerry Finn, the university's oldest alumnus, has sullied the scheduled Centenarian Award by being a party to this.

Straight from the campus daily newspaper of what was once the most revered Catholic university in the world. No longer. Talk about inciting Town and Gown. We hoped Gerry hadn't seen it.

We went back and reread the editorial a few times. "Stem useful engagement and dialogue"? Doubletalk. And "stem"? Surely someone must have seen the implication of that word in that context.

There was, of course, no footnote or disclaimer to inform readers that editorial content of *The Observer* had, for almost a year now, been subject to the review and approval of a "Unification Board." Under the supervision of the university president.

Meanwhile, Father Fischer was playing his role of campus counterspy to the hilt. He arranged with Shelby to meet him at the Grotto at noon on Wednesdays. As they knelt at the praying gate in that holy and halcyon glade of Our Lady, he would surreptitiously pass her a folded single page. It would have been far easier to simply drop it in the mail to us, but Father Fischer must have been a John le Carré or Tom Sawyer fan. Drama was everything.

We were grateful for his help and through him we learned that HIP (Henry Ignatius Pankey) was indeed at sixes and sevens as far as how to respond to an increasing number of media queries. He told us that first amendment and media litigators from the university's Chicago legal firm of Moore & Moore were ever-present.

The *South Bend Sentinel* and our Titanic Team had become the darlings of more than a few campus and national pro-life organizations that had sprung up last year to assail the university for its invitation and honoring of Mubaraq El Baba.

With minor exceptions, other well-known Catholic colleges, however, remained quietly on the sidelines. To my regret, Stonehill was among them. We had strong support from the newly formed *Act For Aquinas*, dedicated to promoting Catholicity among universities. Their letters to Father Pankey and the Board of Fellows went unanswered (surprise!) and efforts to interview him fell on fallow ground.

Shelby arrived at my door one evening strangely reserved. We hugged and drove to Gino's in Mishawaka for some fettuccine Alfredo.

"What gives?" I asked her. "I can't get two words out of you tonight."

"How about three words?" she said. "Like Nanette, Faith, and Denise?"

It took a while, but we sorted it out. Three good Catholic ladies I knew from my near-monastic past. One in New York, one in Connecticut, and one in Massachusetts. They'd been following it all, saw my name, eventually called the university, and wound up in Sports Info.

Nanette was planning a *Titanic* dinner party and asked if I could get Gerry Finn to attend. Faith was out of work but willing to fly at her own expense to South Bend and "help out." Denise just wanted to get some quotes from Gerry and me for her blog. It took a while and two glasses of Chianti to convince Shelby I wasn't an interstate lecher.

Our pro-life side was receiving some unexpected backing from a number of *Titanic* Web sites, including one called Club705.org (there were 705 survivors) that was popular with the descendants of those whom the *Carpathia* had rescued.

"705 Plus One!" they crowed on their homepage.

"Welcome, Gerry Finn! One-hundred years later!"

Another site, dedicated to Edward Smith, captain of the *Titanic*, listed all twelve women who were pregnant on the ship and what happened to their children. Where they got their information was a mystery to us, but Gerry Finn was listed as the only one among them still alive. They said it right:

"He Was on the *Titanic* and He's Still Alive!

That Makes Him—Guess What?—a Survivor!!"

Chapter 30

It was now common knowledge that Shelby and I had been the architects and prime movers behind the revelation that ND's oldest alum had, *de facto,* been aboard the *Titanic.* We were both growing thick skins. Shelby continued in her job in Sports Info, ignoring the cold shoulders she received from a few of her colleagues.

"Talk about finding out who your friends are," she told me. "The guy who's nicest to me these days is Hesse. Maybe we misjudged him."

"Guilty conscience," I said.

In my new job with the *Sentinel,* I spent a lot of time on campus trying to evaluate the ND baseball team and this year's Big East schedule. They'd changed coaches last year but had still struggled to climb out of the cellar. They'd been eliminated early in the last two years' post-season tournaments. During mid-March spring break, I was allowed to watch their practices but not talk to the new coach or any of his charges. That didn't stop me from interviewing a lot of guys I knew from previous teams. Most of them told me the truth. It made for more readable copy. Frankly, I was surprised that Hankey Pankey hadn't put me on his No Trespassing list. Well, maybe he had.

I returned home one Tuesday evening to find Shelby on the sidewalk in front of my apartment. She was in the arms of a heavily bearded guy who was clutching her like she was his last lifeline. It was not a sight I'd expected to see. Then I noticed a familiar black Expedition parked at the curb.

In no time, I was hugging him too. Paul Doucette, looking like a castaway from some Pacific island. We huddled together like the last three people on earth, consoling each other.

"It's been more than two months, and it feels like it happened yesterday," Paul said. "I sold my house and just walked. New Hampshire, Maine, Vermont. All kinds of lousy weather. The cops picked me up twice. I told them I'd hear their confession. I know there's no getting over Heidi. Ever. But I thought I'd be better off back here, where she had happy times.

"I was drinking coffee one icy Sunday in a country store in Bennington, Vermont, when I heard the guy on the radio talking about Gerry Finn. Congratulations to you both. Now the world knows. Anyway, the gal behind the counter told me a local resident named Charlie Jones died in the *Titanic* disaster.

"'They recovered his body and he's buried just down the road,' she said. I slip-slid down to the Congregational Church and, sure enough, there was his gravesite. His house is still standing too. I took a few photos. If I can do anything to help you guys see this through, let me know. I work cheap."

"Well, Paul," I said. "Your timing is great. Gerry Finn's son Don is driving him down Saturday, St. Pat's Day. They'll be arriving in the morning and staying at the Morris Inn. The *Sentinel* is staging a "Shake Hands with History" picnic lunch at, appropriately, St. Patrick's County Park. We've got a gazillion folks who want to meet him. And I can't begin to tell you how happy Shelby and I are to see you."

Father Fischer failed to show for his weekly Wednesday rendezvous with Shelby the next day. Her attempts to reach him by phone failed. It was not a good sign. He'd been a big help to us but it appeared that something had gone wrong. The lines were drawn anyway. We wondered just how far our detractors would go to rock the boat.

By ten o'clock Saturday morning, the *Sentinel's* "Shake Hands with History" event at St. Pat's County Park was SRO. More than a thousand Finn fans swarmed around the pavilion waiting to shake hands with a man who'd been swimming in his mother's amniotic fluid while she swam in the freezing North Atlantic. We'd only anticipated five-hundred. Many carried pro-life signs. A dozen or so anti-lifers wandered around with signboards. It was all very civil, but there was one major problem.

Gerry's son Don had called me on my cell at 9:30 to say that El Baba's civilian Security thugs had detained him and his father. Their SUV with the power wheelchair lift had been "booted." No explanation had been given other than that the vehicle's registration number was on a computerized State Department "Watch" list.

He called again and said there was no way they'd make it in time. We bit the bullet, turned on the P.A. system, gave everyone the bad news, and apologized. Then we began grilling hot dogs and hamburgers and handing out soft drinks and Finn-Frisbees while playing Celine Dion pouring out the sound track from *Titanic the Musical.*

Not until mid-afternoon did they arrive at the Morris Inn. Paul Doucette, Jack Graney from the *Sentinel*, Mike Meaney, Shelby, and I were there to greet them. It was a very tired Gerry, but he didn't waste any time gunning his "Swifty" down to the Grotto even before checking in. We all regrouped in the lobby briefly before they went to their room.

"Where's Dorothy?" Mike asked.

"I gave her the day off," said Gerry.

"Tell us about this business with El Baba's storm troopers," I said.

"They claimed it was just a mix-up," said Don. "But I can tell you that it wasn't. I'm always very alert to what's behind me, and there was a black car with three antennas tailing us all the way from Gerry's place. It turned off about a mile before we hit the state line. They were watching for us. We were obviously set up. Four hours we sat there! They extorted—no other word for it—$400 from us. And they treated us like scum."

"You know," said Gerry, "I've never been a political animal. It just isn't interesting. But I have some card-playing friends who are in the thick of it. Just after noon I remembered one of them and I called him. Less than fifteen minutes later, they took the boot off the car and let us go. Like freeing two caged squirrels."

"Can you tell us your friend's name?" I asked.

"Josh, I cannot. I could be wrong about it all. But I do know he's a pal of another guy who packs a lot of weight in Washington. But as I say, I could be wrong."

Gerry napped and we met them again in a few hours. Jessica and another employee from the alumni office joined us for a light dinner in Sorin's. With some embarrassment, she told us that the planned half-time ceremony for Gerry had been downgraded simply to the award of a certificate signed by the Reverend Pankey. No coin toss, no comments by Gerry over the PA system, no mention of the *Titanic*.

"President Pankey sees this game with Stonehill as a major milestone in the history of the congregation. It's the 170th anniversary of Notre Dame's founding. To the month. He wants to use the time to talk about the academic distinction of ND and the seven other CSC colleges. 'Eight for Excellence,' he's calling it. Father Maloney, Stonehill president, will also speak." She looked disconsolate. "I'm sorry."

"Thank heaven for that," Gerry said. "Nobody wants to hear a hundred-year-old bean-counter babbling on about his infirmities. Thank you, Jessica. I'm feeling relieved."

The rest of us were not relieved. In fact, I was mighty ticked off.

"Good thing Dorothy isn't here to hear this," said Meaney.

Jessica turned. "Dorothy?"

"Gerry's daughter," I said. "She brooks no nonsense as they say. Well, you'll forgive me, Jessica, but Father Pankey's ideas on this are pure nonsense. And no mention of Gerry being on *Titanic*? Sounds to me like he's just trying to sidestep the issue of when life begins. Again."

"No check," our waitress told us as she kissed Gerry much to everyone's delight. He "Swiftied" while we walked down to Howard Hall, his old residence freshman year. Most students had yet to return from spring break, but he got a lot of attention from those who were there and he was enjoying himself.

On Sunday morning, we all sat in the basilica for the folk choir mass at 11:45, and then crossed over to the South Dining Hall for brunch. A wide banner hung above one of the doors of the dining hall. Fat green capital letters.

WELCOME GERRY FINN
ND'S OLDEST GRADUATE
AND TITANIC SURVIVOR
YOU'RE OUR GUY!!!!!!!!!

A small group of students applauded as we approached. Some were singing "Cheer, Cheer, for old Gerry Finn ..." Gerry stopped his Swifty next to them and grasped a shapely, blonde-haired girl by the hand. "In case you don't know the second verse to that, it goes like this: "Cheer, cheer for old Gerry Finn. May Mary forgive him for his lifetime of sin ..." The girl, a very, very pretty one, leaned down and kissed him. "Not likely," she laughed. I thanked her and was rewarded with a kiss. Shelby fake-frowned and waved her index finger at me.

But it was a great photo op and we got it. Banner overhead. Cute gal. Gerry smiling. Other students reaching out to touch him. "Swifty" center stage. (Joe Swift, ND '70, must be happy about all this.) Caption: *"Titanic* survivor cheered at Notre Dame." *Put it on our 'send' list in the morning. Father Pankey will love it. Well, maybe not.*

Chapter 31

April 14, 2012, a full century since RMS *Titanic* took more than 1,500 people two and a half miles to the bottom of the North Atlantic.

In Springfield, MA, Missouri's eighty-six-year-old Mary Dolan Jamieson was one of several honored guests (and speakers) at the Titanic Society's milestone convention and unveiling of a new Centennial Memorial. The weekend program included a Saturday afternoon teleconference with Gerry Finn. It was a last-minute arrangement prompted by the publication, a week earlier, of an editorial in the *Wall Street Journal*. For us, the editorial was a godsend. For Father Pankey, less so.

ND Disputes Finn Claim;
WSJ Research Disputes ND

One-hundred years after the sinking of the ill-fated RMS *Titanic*, the University of Notre Dame's president said the portrayal of Gerard Finn, the school's oldest alumnus, as the last survivor "is well-intentioned but a bit of a fanciful tale."

The Reverend Henry I. Pankey said that "There is really no valid documentation to support the claim by the *South Bend Sentinel* newspaper" and "the topic of the sanctity of life is not at issue here."

"This entire episode is the consequence of a well-intentioned but overly enthusiastic attempt by several *Sentinel* employees to publicize Mr. Finn's 100th birthday.

"We don't consider a questionable birth certificate and somewhat blurred photograph sufficient to support this imaginative scenario. Mr. Finn is a wonderful man and held in very high regard by this university. We intend to honor his centennial at a home game on Nov. 3. But it's clear that under no circumstance could he be considered to have been a passenger on *Titanic*."

Recent inquiries by the *Journal*, however, have turned up reinforcing and credible evidence showing otherwise. Details from a 100-year-old document list Finn's mother as one of a dozen expectant women onboard.

Journal staffers have located a "List or Manifest of Alien Passengers for the United States" compiled aboard the Cunard Line rescue ship *Carpathia* before it arrived in New York on April 18, 1912. The list, found only a week ago in Cunard's archives, clearly shows the entry "Kate Curran Finn, with child."

South Bend Sentinel publisher Ken Fromac said, "In the opinion of this newspaper and in the opinion of medical science and intelligent human beings, an *in utero* child is a person. Gerard Finn was most certainly a passenger on the ship. How else did he arrive here? Can someone tell me? As such, he is indeed the last survivor of that terrible night."

Notre Dame's Pankey professed to have no knowledge of the Cunard Line document, but insisted that it changes nothing. "Some people are trying to turn this into a theological issue. It serves no purpose."

Paul, Shelby, Mike, Jack Graney, and I spent the April 14 weekend in Chicago, lending support to Gerry for his Saturday afternoon teleconference with the *Titanic* celebrants in Massachusetts. In Springfield, Mary Dolan introduced him to a cheering crowd as "The man I've yet to meet but I may marry him."

Gerry didn't need any coaching for the somewhat clamorous interview. His ninety-nine years of life and two months of recent sparring with the media had given him an easy-going presence that connected with just about anyone, including his skeptics—and there were many. Tongue in cheek, he fielded questions from *Titanic* aficionados some eight hundred miles distant.

Q. "Mr. Flynn, have you ever had any major medical problems?"
A. "It's Finn, as in fish. But double 'n'. At my age I expect everyone to get my name right. I hope you won't be engraving my tombstone."
Q. "Sorry. Well, have you? Major medical problems?"
A. "When I was six. Spanish flu. I thought I was a goner. Fifty million people died but the good Lord let me live. Just so I could be here tonight and be called Mr. Flynn."
Q. "Do you honestly consider yourself a survivor?"
A. "I don't do anything dishonestly. And yes, I was as much on board that ship as John Jacob Astor and Molly Brown. Anyone who had told my mom I wasn't there would have had his hands full, believe me."
Q. "How did you manage to live so long?"
A. "I didn't fall down and didn't stop breathing. Didn't smoke and drank in moderation. Lots of naps—and it helps to be a sports nut."
Q. "Are you still a Cub's fan?"
A. "You didn't see me out there on the mound at Wrigley on opening day? They clocked me at thirty-seven miles per hour. That's better than a lot of guys making ten million bucks in that league. They made me an offer, but I'm just too busy."
Silence. Then:
Q. "Think you can make it to another hundred?"
A. "Could be, but right now I'm enjoying it all. You could say I'm sucking the marrow out of the bones of life."

There was much more and afterward Gerry took a nap while his daughter Dorothy prepared a commemorative "Steerage Special" of rice soup, corned beef, and cabbage, boiled potatoes and peaches and rice. The same fare that third-class passengers ate on that fateful night. We downed it all with gusto and a couple of bottles of merlot. Gerry told us that a check for $400 had been delivered anonymously to him, the exact amount extorted on St. Patrick's Day by El Baba's checkpoint citizen soldiers. The envelope also contained an MB (Muslim Brother) license plate sticker. Gerry said he had a graphics-savvy friend convert it to BM.

Later, in Paul's Expedition, we detoured once more from the toll road to avoid El Baba's hooligans on our way back to South Bend. This was, of course, a presidential election year, and we learned later that the thugs manning the Fed's checkpoints had added a new twist. Vehicles passing through a toll station lane were being halted at random as one of the "Nasties" slapped a "Re-Elect El Baba! Jobs & Justice!" sticker on its back bumper.

I had five messages on my phone tape when I returned home. I'd fallen far behind in my personal life. This was the last weekend to send in tax returns for last year and, like most Americans, it brought me face to face with the actual consequences of the draconian laws enacted two years earlier by our Marxist administration. For me, it meant a painful 10 percent hike in my adjusted gross income that spiked me into a higher bracket, but for others it was much worse. I wondered if Gerry, at age ninety-nine, was still preparing returns for his friends as he had done for so many years.

Three of my five incoming calls were from Leo Darcy, an ND grad and the guy who had organized *Act For Aquinas* to reverse the increasing secularization of Catholic colleges in America. Leo was planning to release a public statement on behalf of AFA to address the comments of Father Pankey in the *Wall Street Journal*. Could I make sure the *Sentinel* played it up?

You bet.

("Wouldn't you have thought," confided Leo, "that he'd enough savvy to turn that call from the *Journal* over to his communications folks? Apparently, he just picked up the phone himself and answered their questions. Said they'd done a fine story on him before, so he expected another one.")

Leo's disputes with Father Pankey on secularization and embryonic stem cell research had been one-sided to this point. The university president either considered himself above the fray or simply didn't care about public or Church opinion. In any case, all of AFA's letters, e-mails, and communications had been totally ignored by the Board of Fellows.

"No more than a political action committee," pooh-poohed Pankey.

The AFA's strong representation among a lot of ND alumni seemed to matter not a whit.

Another of my calls was from Father Fred Fischer, resurrected, it appeared, from oblivion. "Call me as soon as you get this," he said. I did so. No answer. The last call was from a testy ND coed named Lisa Walters, president of the ND for Animals Alliance. I listened briefly to her tirade. ("People worry more about their unborn babies than they do about their living pets!") I hung up. *Lisa, send your camel to bed.*

I sat and thought about the day and about Gerry. All of this has to be taking its toll on him. I said a quick prayer to his guardian the Blessed Mother that he would continue to be up to it, and I was getting into bed when the phone rang. Father Fischer.

"A heads-up, Josh. Our president has been in a bit of a frenzy since that *Journal* editorial. He's looking for some targets and I think you're one of them. You can expect a summons very soon. He'll probably have some of the other Fellows sit in."

"Thanks, Father. Did he forget he already got rid of me? I'll enjoy this. I might even sue him. Appreciate your call and we'll talk soon. A belated Happy St. Patrick's Day to you."

I went to bed happy. I was becoming an annoyance to the powers-that-be. *What more can I do to make them the powers-that-were?* Whatever, I was not about to take any more guff. Ruff, ruff.

Chapter 32

Shelby, Mike Meaney, Paul Doucette, and I went into a huddle at St. Mary's Lake after Sunday's 10 AM liturgical choir mass. I'd invited Paul to accompany me to 400 Main Building Monday at 2 PM, the appointed time of my meeting with the Reverend Pankey and his colleagues, one male and one female.

"Very strange," said Paul. "I suspect a trap. No offense, Josh, but why would he waste his time on you? If the president has something of substance to say, why wouldn't he dump it on some lamestream media groupie? They love him and they love to grovel."

"Except for the *Sentinel* and the *Journal*," I reminded him. "We'll just see how it goes. I think he just wants to vent his spleen. He can't believe everyone doesn't revere him."

I remembered my visit to Joe Gallagher, squinted my eyes, and growled in my best George Smiley imitation. "Think I should wear a wire, Mike?"

"How about this, Josh?" said Paul. "I'll come along and I'll be carrying a recorder. Out in the open. You'll have a backup in your pocket. They'll scream bloody murder so I'll leave. But you'll still have yours."

It happened exactly that way.

"Who is this, Allen? And what's he doing with that recorder?" the Reverend Pankey fired at me when we entered his spacious office Monday afternoon.

"This is Paul Doucette. He's acting as my lawyer. Pankey."

"It's Father Pankey to you. And Doucette is no lawyer. He's one of our well-known drop-outs."

"Yes, and it's *Mister* Allen to you."

Father Pankey's face turned the color of ashes. No doubt he hadn't encountered such disrespect in all of his fifty-seven years.

A tall, thin woman with a pinched mouth, towering teeth and a horsy countenance stood and extended a hand to Paul and me. "I'm Louise Van der Horst. I'm chairperson of the university relations and PR committee. Thank you for coming, Mr. Allen and Mr. Doucette."

She pointed to a rotund, unsmiling man sitting next to her. He did not rise. "And this is Mr. Trevor Boatwright, recently of Yale University and an accomplished scholar. Mr. Boatwright now chairs our committee on social values and responsibilities. We three are Fellows of the university, as you no doubt are aware."

He grunted and I just nodded.

"Now we don't want you gentlemen to feel intimidated this afternoon," she continued, "and we hope we can maintain a proper decorum in our conversation. We seem to have gotten off to a poor start there."

"Mr. Doucette will be leaving," Father Pankey announced, "and so will his tape recorder. I trust it is not activated. We have only a few questions for Allen here."

Apparently, the university president had not been tuned in to Ms. Van der Horst's call for proper decorum. I stood. "It's either Mr. Allen and Father Pankey, or it's Allen and Pankey. Your choice." Father Pankey's cherubic face clouded over and his blue eyes raged.

"Please," said Mrs. (Ms.?) VDH. "Let us put an end to this pique, to this rancor. And Mr. Doucette, I'm sorry, but you will have to leave if we are to continue."

Pankey pique, Pankey rancor. I could write a song around that.

Paul shut the door quietly behind him. My recorder was running quietly in my inside jacket pocket. I'd hoped to pass some of whatever this group had to say along to Leo Darcy with the *Act For Aquinas* group. So far that had been nothing.

Without even looking in my direction, bandy-legged, Trevor-late-of-Yale spoke up:

"It's quite simple, young fellow, we just need to know why you continue to pursue some will-o'-the-wisp delusion about this fellow Finn."

It seemed that Trevor had fallen in love with the word "fellow." Now that he was one, academically speaking.

I was beyond caring. "Well, old fellow," I said, "perhaps it's because that fellow Finn was on that ship just as surely as you and I are here today playing word games in Notre Dame's Main Building."

Silence. There were no words to describe my impertinence.

"Mr. Allen, let's start over," said Ms. (Mrs.?) VDH. "What we're implying is that all of this continuing publicity about Mr. Finn comes at a price. To this university's Catholic reputation. It goes without saying that we are pro-life and we believe that life begins at conception. There are, of course, a great many who believe otherwise and who don't consider a fetus a person. Father Pankey has done much privately and publicly to demonstrate our commitment to the sanctity of life. However, this continuing barrage of demands from the media is distracting us, to say the least, from administering to the needs of students and supporters.

"There is one quick way to resolve this problem, and we trust your newspaper will be agreeable."

She picked up a folder and extracted a piece of paper. "This is datelined here and we would like to release it as soon as possible." She began reading.

> NOTRE DAME, IN, April 18, 2012 —Reverend Henry I. Pankey, President of Notre Dame University and a member of the American Academy of Arts and Sciences, today signed a certificate honoring Mr. Gerard Finn of Chicago as the university's first centenarian. The certificate will be presented on his 100th birthday, Nov. 3, when the Fighting Irish host Stonehill College.
>
> Mr. Finn has attained celebrity status lately. His mother, Catherine Finn, immigrated to the United States in 1912, surviving the *Titanic* disaster. The achievements of mother and son have received worldwide recognition in recent months.

"We're most proud of Mr. Finn," said Reverend Pankey, "and we plan to continue working in conjunction with the *South Bend Sentinel* newspaper to honor his unique status."

I put my hand out and she gave me a copy. It was a non-story, a no-news news story, one of hundreds that float across newsrooms daily and disappear in disgrace into a black hole.

Its only reason for existing (however unstated) was to slyly imply university support of the fact that Gerry was considered a *Titanic* survivor. Hence, unstudied readers might deduce that Notre Dame viewed a three-month fetus as a person. Of course, it was flat-out fiction that they had been working in conjunction with the *Sentinel*. And their need for our approval of that fabrication was the only reason I'd been summoned here.

They would like it both ways.

"This is your release, of course, Ms. Van der Horst," I told her. "But you must see that it is only inviting the obvious follow-up question you will get from anyone and everyone in the media. 'So the university believes that Gerry Finn as a three-month fetus was also a passenger on the ship?' Trust me, no journalist would be content with this, unless he or she was the editor of your student *Observer*. It simply begs more questions."

"Mr. Allen, let me be the judge of that. I have some thirty years experience—extensive—in the communications arena, both print and broadcast. I know what to feed those people."

Trevor the Clever was nodding vehemently. It occurred to me that there might be a lucrative market for Board of Fellows bobbleheads.

I put the copy in my pocket, fully aware that the professionals in the university's communications department must be running for their lives from all this. *If it had even been shared with them.*

"Before I go, you said that the university believes that life begins at conception. Are you aware that one of your prominent theology professors just a few years ago said exactly the opposite in a published article? She was speaking for Notre Dame, wouldn't you say? She was arguing in favor of embryonic stem cell research. If the university continues to sidestep the issue of whether or not Finn was a passenger on that ship, then your silence is tacit approval of her views.

"As for this release, I'll have to get back to you, of course. Our publisher will need to see it. Incidentally, Gerry's mother spelled her first name with a K. Not a C."

"Mr. Allen," said Father Pankey, conceding for the first time that I (if not the infant Gerry Finn) was a real person, "this has really gone on far too long. We do not expect any delay on this. We need to get this out. We are not without authority, not without power, as you well know."

"I do indeed, Father. I remember being unjustly separated from my employment here. February sixth. The birthday of your founder, Father Edward Sorin. In case you didn't know, Father Sorin advised his peers that the university should never attempt to discipline someone by expelling him. Let him just resign, he said. He might come back one day to exact retribution. Some students have a way of later embarrassing the institutions that turn them out.

"Not his precise words, but you get the idea."

They were all looking at me in amazement. I headed for the door, waving their single page of wretched, crippled words. "It won't be more than a day, Father."

My bosses at the *Sentinel* just shook their heads when I showed it to them. "Pure pabulum," said Jack Graney. He snatched it from my hand and ran a black felt-tip pen through the last eighteen words. "Don't they have a course in honesty out there?" he asked me.

"They don't think it necessary."

He initialed his edit and gave it back to me. "Make a copy and send it back to them. Amateur night at the Bijou."

I couldn't do it fast enough.

A week passed with no release forthcoming from the campus. It occurred to me that we had saved them considerable embarrassment. But Leo Darcy with *Act For Aquinas* took a page from the current White House playbook and didn't let a serious crisis go to waste. And the *Wall Street Journal* editorial contradicting Father Pankey had indeed brought a serious crisis down upon the haughty heads of the university's Fellows. They were now officially on record as denying a basic tenet of the Catholic Church: that life begins at conception.

Darcy seized the day. His widely distributed comments on AFA letterhead made a strong case that generated a lot of headlines and Internet play. He said this, in part:

After some two months of dodging the issue, the Reverend Henry I. Pankey, president of Notre Dame University, has abrogated any public assumption that the school, once considered the cradle of Catholic academic excellence in this country, would categorically define a human organism as distinct from its parents, as a human individual and, hence, as much a human person as if carried in his mother's arms.

Father Pankey's recent statement to the *Wall Street Journal* made that very clear when he said "under no circumstance could he (Gerry Finn) be considered to have been a passenger on Titanic."

At the same time, however, *Act For Aquinas* has learned that another member of the university's governing Board of Fellows only last week asserted "It goes without saying that we are pro-life and we believe that life begins at conception."

Apparently, it does go without saying. But it also seems that those who now control ND are not singing from the same hymnal.

I knew Leo's comments would be sure to stoke the flames in the Main Building, but I had Ms. Van der Horst's words on tape and I had been happy to share them with him.

Chapter 33

Notre Dame's 167th commencement was held on May 20 in the stadium. Shelby and I were among the twenty thousand sitting in the warm Sunday sunshine to hear honored (and dreadlocked) speaker DeRon Dontelle lecture, in somewhat stern terms, three thousand graduates and families on the need to share their assets and resources with the oppressed and less fortunate.

DeRon (now Dr. DeRon Dontelle following the university's award of an honorary Doctor of Laws) had not submitted his speech in advance as was usually done for publicity purposes. Indeed, it was obvious that DeRon had not bothered to prepare a speech. His remarks were, as one might say, off the cuff. And cuffs were something with which he was familiar, having served several prison terms for a variety of felonies in between his activities as a big-name NBA player.

"Let us all learn from Dr. Dontelle this morning," intoned Father Pankey. *"Let us all take something away from this man whose resiliency you would all do well to emulate, a man whose bootstrap credentials have brought him to where he is today ..."*

"There was a time," I whispered to Shelby, "when a commencement ceremony at Notre Dame was actually dignified. All we're lacking here today is a transgender streaker. What are they thinking of?"

But these were deemed days of compassion, diversity, and social righteousness by ND's Board of Fellows. In that spirit and in their persistent PC posturing, they had presumably reasoned that DeRon's presence on campus would somehow funnel more DC dollars to the Dome.

They had, of course, closed their eyes and ears tightly to the lingering, problematic "ND88" case shrieking for justice from their own locked closet.

The day would be remembered by many as the "Put up some dough for them you don't know!" commencement address. It was an appeal that, however grammatically ruptured, sprung repeatedly from the ringed lips of Dr. Dontelle for an agonizing hour or more.

It mattered not, however, that much of what he had to say that morning was lost forever. It was simply unintelligible. But given the loud and lasting applause that rocked the stadium for a full five minutes following, one would have thought that Knute Rockne, George Gipp, and Johnny Lujack had suddenly appeared mid-field, holding hands.

We're looking at more than the transformation of America, I thought. *Now we're looking at the undeniable transformation of a university that was founded only sixty-six years after this nation's birth.*

Shelby and I fled to St. Mary's Lake for solace. I found it difficult to even comment, but apparently Shelby had been busy being creative.

"How's this?" she asked.

> For help with speaking or how to spell,
> Such difficult words as 'parallel,'
> Remember this and remember it well
> Don't ask, don't ask, don't ask Dontelle.

I swallowed a laugh. "For shame, Shelby. And all that time I thought you were listening."

I just hoped that this day would be long forgotten by the time I re-entered the stadium on September 8 for ND's home opener with Purdue.

Last month's eighty-third Blue-Gold scrimmage, marking the end of four weeks' spring practice, left optimists optimistic and pessimists pessimistic. The Irish defense appeared porous, kicking was mediocre, and the offensive line was perhaps one level below what many hoped for. But the key quarterback slot seemed to be solid.

ND coach Sean Noonan's not-so-secret weapon, as the football world knew, was junior Shaquel Walker from San Leandro, CA, a wide receiver whose more than 2,000 yards in 2011 left him just shy of an NCAA single-season Division 1-A record.

The price of a ticket to the Blue-Gold game now ranged from twenty five dollars to one hundred fifty dollars depending on one's desires to rub notable elbows at peripheral VIP events. The money flowed downstream to provide scholarships for Michiana area students.

Eight-hundred miles to the east, the Stonehill College football team had ended its own spring practice schedule with its annual Purple-White scrimmage (free admission) at W.B. Mason Stadium. The team would open on September 8 against Connecticut State University, but there was really only one game on their schedule this year and that was November 3 in South Bend.

Skyhawk head coach Rob Leake had been having digestive problems for seven months now. A game against the Fighting Irish was the last thing he'd ever anticipated when he signed on at SC six years ago. Behind his enthusiastic, happy-go-lucky patina, he lay awake nights wondering if he was being punished for some youthful transgression.

Despite the Skyhawks' winning record last year, it would take nothing short of a miracle for his charges to move the ball against the Irish. ND's defensive line had an average forty-pound weight advantage and Leake had no idea how to get around that. Whatever offensive hopes he had rested on the broad shoulders of junior Tyler Smith who, despite his 235 pounds, could do forty yards in 4.5 seconds. Smith stood five feet nine and had topped the NE-10 Conference last year in yards rushing. He was healthy, but Leake wanted to put him in a glass bubble with a "Do Not Open Until November 2" label.

The enthusiasm for football under the Golden Dome that Shelby and I normally felt at this time of year was on the wane, no doubt a consequence of our skirmishes with Father Pankey and the hardnosed stance of the university on the issue of life. I'd decided that all things considered, I'd be cheering for Stonehill while covering the Irish for the *Sentinel*.

Meanwhile, we needed to get our ducks in a row for Gerry's annual class reunion trip down at the end of this month. He and his son Don would be here from Thursday through Sunday, June 3. But it was not to be.

Chapter 34

Jessica from the alumni office called me at the *Sentinel* Monday afternoon. "It's Gerry. He has some sort of circulatory problem and he's in Sacred Heart Hospital. Dorothy said he's lucid and complaining, so I suppose that's good. No diagnosis yet. Obviously he won't be down next week. But you might want to hold up on getting the news out. He's a tough guy."

"When did you find out?"

"She called us a little while ago. Asked that I tell everyone. She said, 'Don't plan on visiting. Or sending anything.' She'll keep us posted. The EMTs took him this morning about ten. So be careful. Bad things happen in threes and that's number two."

"What was number one?"

"Yesterday's commencement."

It was very upsetting news and I didn't like the idea of not visiting him. "Don't worry, Josh," Shelby told me that night. "People don't die of old age. No such thing. Besides, I think our gal Mary down in Missouri is setting her cap for Gerry. Mary and Gerry. Into the sunset together. Does that give you any ideas?"

"What?"

"Nothing."

Surprisingly, Gerry's trip to the hospital remained undetected by the press. He was released only three days later with the usual instructions and follow-up. "Take your meds, keep in touch, and stick close to your nest." He was advised to let friends and family handle all communications. I vowed to call him at least once a week.

Alumni reunion came and went without much hoopla. There was only one alumnus from any classes in the '30s and just two from the year 1940. Father Pankey's comments at the closing alumni weekend dinner carefully avoided any reference to Gerry or the *Titanic* issue. Those who expected otherwise were disappointed.

Mike Meaney, whose class was celebrating its sixtieth anniversary, filled us in on Pankey's remarks.

"Same old, same old," he said. "There were three of us from '52. We all felt like throwing up. The man talked about being 'distinctly Catholic' but not letting religion stand in the way of seeking social justice for all. What the hell does that mean? It has to be confusing to anyone. Seems like we're getting to be a clone of liberal Protestantism. Not what Father Sorin had in mind."

Gerry and the *Titanic* were becoming lukewarm topics on the Internet and in the media. We tried our best to keep the story alive, but it seemed that the Reverend Pankey had escaped without his feet really being held to the fire. Even worse, some east coast scholarly association affiliated with Trinity College in Dublin had named him its "Irish Academic Progressive of the Year." A lot of preening and puffery from various campus sources followed that one. I was all in favor of burying it on the *Sentinel's* classified ad page, but that, of course, was not in my bailiwick and it ran on page one.

I was still getting a few e-mails and phone calls on the "Last Survivor" topic, some insistent on getting Gerry to speak at one convention or another. I'd also received a couple of more calls from the animal rights coed Lisa Walters. Unfortunately for me she lived just up the road in Niles and wanted to meet me and explain her concerns. I was polite, but no more.

The days slipped by and the great celestial conjunction of the summer solstice was at hand. I tried my best to understand it all but could only grasp that this was just a preview of the upcoming "Doomsday" conjunction to occur on December 21. Bad energy soon to be streaming down from above on us earthlings.

Our friend Father Fischer had totally disappeared from the campus and no one had any intelligence on his absence. Where had he gone?

Hopefully not to the Pakistani mission where Father Dick Novak, CSC and a student at both ND and Stonehill, had been murdered in the 60s.

I seemed to be getting bad vibes about everything. I called my old friend Father Donahue at Stonehill. He planned to attend the game on November 3 but was having trouble finding a room. I told him he could stay with me or maybe Paul Doucette who had taken up permanent residence at "Heidi House."

I had no lunch plans that day, but someone else did. The guard called from the lobby.

"Josh, there's a young lady down here who would like to speak to you about Gerry Finn. Says it's important."

She looked very familiar. And very pretty.

She came forward and seized my hand as I got off the elevator. I recognized her as the coed who had kissed both Gerry and me in front of the chow hall that day. A low-cut pink summer frock and a flower in her blond hair. She could have just stepped off the cover of *Health & Fitness*.

"I'm taking you to lunch, Josh, and don't say no. Fresh summer salad, crab legs, and baked Alaska. You will want to marry me."

I was too stunned to speak.

We walked. Not one block or two, but eight. I had to sprint to keep up. The Pagan Vegan had a daily, no-meat menu printed on what looked like one of those white cardboards that once came in laundered shirts. It was topped by a childish sketch showing a dark line descending at an angle from a cluster of dots to a six-armed sun.

"That's today," she explained. "The summer solstice. The alignment of our sun between the bull's horns. The Pleiades. That's what I'm doing today, you see. Taking the bull by the horns."

"You have the advantage of me," I said. "I don't even know your name. But your voice is somehow familiar."

"As well it should be. My name is Lisa Walters and I think maybe I will marry you. You're a lot nicer than you were on the telephone. And I know you and that redhead are a pair. But you'll like me better. I wanted to apologize to you. I certainly don't think pets are more important than unborn babies. It just all came out wrong. A lot of my friends on campus think you walk on water. Do you?"

It was a sun-splattered solstice I would remember. But not happily. By the time we ambled (she ambled, I trudged) the eight blocks back to the *Sentinel*, I was almost an hour late and feeling like I'd been kidnapped. But to say I didn't enjoy it would be a lie.

"We'll do this again, Josh," she said in the lobby. "You can be sure of that." She kissed me again and was gone. Gary the guard looked at me and shook his head. He knew me and he knew Shelby. Well.

Everyone in South Bend must have seen me having that solstice lunch with Ms. Walters. Maybe even taken pictures. When I picked Shelby up on Saturday evening (she'd begged off with a headache Friday night), she was wearing a blond wig, a V-neck puffy pink dress, and what looked like an entire tube of lipstick. She didn't have to say anything and I didn't know what to say. I laughed, but she didn't.

"Are we going out with you looking like that?" I asked.

"Like what?"

"Like Krusty the Clown."

"It's my Suzi Summer solstice costume. Very much in vegan vogue these days."

"Shelby ..."

"Yes?"

"I was shanghaied. I didn't even know that girl's name."

"I'm sure you do now."

"I ..."

"Yes?"

And so it went until I finally turned and left.

Lisa Walters, animal activist, but also a trap-setter, did not call again and I was grateful. However, Shelby avoided me like I was a leper, and it was painful. Not a lot of sleep. I stopped calling. Pride is a perverse sin. *We've come so far ... how could we let it slip away?*

June evaporated quickly into July. Highest summer. The Fourth was a Wednesday and Paul Doucette called me on Monday with an invite.

"I'm having a barbecue. Ribs and bibs. Maybe a G&T or two. No fireworks. Be there at noon. It is only right and just."

The first thing I noticed was that Paul had shaved his beard and had Jessica from the alumni office at his side. They both welcomed me and gave me hugs. The second thing I noticed was Shelby. She smiled.

She was wearing a red, white, and blue top hat that stayed balanced on her head only long enough for me to wrap my arms around her. We left early to the hoots and boos of the neighborhood. But it was time for some serious talk.

"I have a good memory," I said. "I remember what my mom told me, and I've let too many sunsets go by without apologizing."

"Not your fault, Josh. It's my green eyes. Couldn't stand to hear about that little kid going after you. That's what happens when you get close to thirty. Anyway, I cancelled her little cruise with an iceberg of my own."

"We're not getting any younger, Shelby. Do you think your family would put up with a second-rate sportswriter? And do they have any Catholic churches down there in Tidewater?"

"Josh, that sounds suspiciously like a …"

"It is, Shelby. It truly is. Do you remember what Gerry said first time you met him? When he was talking about his wife? It could have been me."

"What did he say?"

"He said, 'But oh, I loved that redhead most of all.'"

Shelby laughed. "Of course I remember. I just wanted to hear you say it."

"Give me time and I'll present you with a miniature down at the Grotto. That's the drill, you know."

"How well I do. I've given it considerable thought, as they say."

"And …?"

She smiled and hugged me. I took that as a "Yes."

Later we sat on her back porch and listened to the tree frogs telegraphing one another.

It was a tender moment and I reached for her hand. "My mom also told me that when the time came, I'd know a real lady when I met her."

She smiled again. "I told that Michigan bitch I'd turn her and her porno-pink frock into confetti if she called you again."

Chapter 35

It was the summer of 2012. The nation, after 235 years as a freedom-loving republic, was now in the chains of something called a New Internationalism, a New World Order, and under the control of the dictator Mabaraq El Baba and his toadies.

In London, Olympiad XXX was cancelled after two days of riots by Muslim terrorists resulting in the death of hundreds. Twenty American tourists were held for questioning.

The state of Arizona no longer existed. It had been ceded in its entirety to Mexico and its former governor and others were being investigated by two Congressional committees for treasonable activity. Citizen dissent had been criminalized.

The fifty-seventh quadrennial presidential election was scheduled for Tuesday, November 6 but had been temporarily suspended by executive order until the Fairness in Immigration Act of 2012 was passed. It was an Orwellian tyranny.

Only seven weeks until the season opener against Navy. It would be played at Croke Park in Dublin where the day's highlight was to be the award of a plaque to Father Henry I. Pankey, honoring him as the "Irish Academic Progressive of the Year."

Meanwhile, the football Irish sandwiched private daily workouts in between their off-campus activities. Two dozen athletes—including ten from the grid squad—were arrested and fined for underage drinking. Their stature seemed to rise on campus while what passed for a student disciplinary authority looked the other way. Team practice didn't actually begin until the second week of August and I was beginning to wish it never would. I was even losing interest in the November 3 contest.

Gerry seemed to have regained his strength and had no further problems with his circulation. Shelby and I were planning our big day, and Father Donahue, who'd be staying with Paul Doucette, had agreed to perform the nuptials. We hadn't decided exactly when and I still had to visit a jewelry store.

I arrived at the *Sentinel* one morning to find an overnight delivery package waiting for me. It was from a woman who managed a nursing home in Shreveport, LA. Inside were a letter and a framed (and autographed) photograph of an elderly black lady. Lemon-yellow jacket, star-shaped earrings, and a yellow pearl necklace. There were other photos and a copy of a certificate signed by the mayor of Shreveport. I read the letter first.

Mr. Allen:
Let us introduce you and Mr. Gerry Finn, and all your friends, to Miss Mississippi Winn, age 115 years and 115 days today, July 24, 2012. Miss Winn is America's oldest living African-American and the sixth oldest person in the world.

Miss (Aunt Sweetie) Winn is still very active and one of Shreveport's best bingo players. She is also a staunch member of our local pro-life Action Group and wants Mr. Finn to know that she is proud to support him.

Also enclosed please find a copy of a certificate of commendation signed by our mayor of Shreveport honoring her.

Is it possible that we may one day expect a Winn-Finn alliance? When we asked her, she replied: "He's too young for me."

It was enough to reaffirm one's faith in the nation. Every once in awhile, there's a really good reason to smile. We all loved it and it dominated the *Sentinel's* mid-week "People" insert. We made copies, repackaged it all and sent it on to Gerry. We had a copy (marked "Of possible interest") delivered to Office #400, Main Building. And we moved it on the wires with photos.

I called the lady from the nursing home in Shreveport and thanked her and "Aunt Sweetie." Then we framed one of Gerry's signed photos and sent that overnight with copies of our *Sentinel* story. In days gone by, we would have also enclosed some Notre Dame memorabilia. But that was in days gone by.

While summer practice for the footballers was foremost on the minds of most ND fans and sportswriters, the Reverend Pankey's staff was busy coordinating a "StaND Against Hate" program for August 14–17. Joining the university president to sponsor these four days of ultra-sexual self-introspection, films, lectures, and mutual encouragement were the Gender Relations Center; the student government; the university's Counseling Center; the Office of Student Affairs; the Core Council for Lesbian, Gay, Bisexual, Transgender and Questioning Students; the Feminist Voice; and the Campus Ministry. A formidable lineup to assist those who couldn't decide which public bathroom to use. And to spread further moral confusion among everyone else.

Chapter 36

A moist, humid Midwest evening, the rain cascading from the downspout, the guttural roll of receding thunder and the trilling of a stiff-tailed Carolina Wren. We sat on Shelby's small porch overlooking the ragged, waterlogged patch of land that she shared with her neighbors.

"This would be a good time to start a soup kitchen," I said sourly. "Nothing to do with altruism or compassion. Just as a moneymaker. Those are the folks who get the lion's share of federal aid now and it will only get better. The people who own real businesses will be the ones patronizing the soup kitchens."

"You're in a cheerful mood tonight."

"Sorry."

Maybe it was just the late August heat, but I couldn't seem to shake a growing feeling of deep depression. Impending doom. But, I assured Shelby, nothing to do with our relationship. That was the bright spot.

"Not at all," I told her. "It's just a feeling of total helplessness. This country is on its deathbed and no one seems to care. They don't believe we're all in danger. Should we be surprised that they've rammed through that so-called Fairness in Immigration Act of 2012? You know what that means. Our Congress does its best work after midnight, just like the burglars they are. Stealing our freedoms, one by one, and nobody bothers to investigate."

"I hate to see you like this, Josh."

"What's more, Shelby, I don't even feel like I'm a part of Notre Dame anymore. I don't understand how they can continue to separate themselves from the Church. They should send in the Swiss Guards and take Pankey out in shackles. Toss him and El Baba in the tower with those two princes."

"You're confusing your geography—and me," she said.

Classes had resumed on the twenty-first, and my friend Brian Hargrove, an old-timer who covered ND football for the *Chicago Tribune*, arrived in town. Like most of the Trib's sports staff, he knew Gerry well and we lamented the fact that the Cubs were eighteen games behind with only thirty-four remaining.

"Maybe we'll get a miracle," I said. "This is the month of the blue moon, you know."

"Think Gerry can hang on another year?"

"I do," I told him. "But I don't know if the Cubs can. Even the ivy is dying. Think the Trib might do a piece on Gerry when he's down here for the Stonehill game? He's supposed to be honored at half time. Supposed to be, but they seem to be making a dog's dinner out of it. No PA announcement or anything, just slip him some piece of paper when no one is watching."

"Josh, I'll be up in the press box among good friends and I guarantee you that there will be an announcement. And it will include the fact that he's a *Titanic* survivor. I know what's going on down here. Let's stay in touch on the details."

"Thanks, Brian. And that's thanks from more people than you can imagine."

All the shamrocks, rainbows, and leprechauns in the greater Dublin area were of no help to the South Bend Irish as they were torpedoed 21-7 by the Naval Academy in their season's opener at Croke Park. They returned to campus on Labor Day, September 3, with little more to show for their 7,200-mile round trip than a gilded plaque honoring Reverend Pankey. The table was not very well set for Saturday's upcoming bout with Purdue. In North Easton, MA, Skyhawk hopes began to slowly ascend. Exactly two months to the Big Day.

I'd told Ed Wagner at Stonehill that Paul, Shelby, and I could accommodate him and some of his friends for that first week of November. No food, but a few beds, sleeping bags, and sofas. With motel rooms going for as high as six hundred dollars a night, it was no surprise we quickly received a list of some twenty-five hopefuls. Could we do it? We could, I told him.

ND gridders struggled through a dismal 2-5 record in September and October, including an embarrassing 24–10 loss to Boston College on Founder's Day, October 13.

Shelby and I were juggling our schedules between work and details of Gerry's birthday commemoration. These were days of diligence. We were on overload. The Board of Fellows may well have downsized the planned celebration for Gerry on game day, but we weren't about to let that pass quietly.

Gerry, his daughter, Dorothy, and son, Don would be staying at the Morris Inn from Thursday through Sunday. The Alumni Association had assigned different grads as *aide-de-camps* for them each day.

We planned a pre-emptive strike. In the past year, we had become well-acquainted with the campus student associations who had the courage to challenge the university's stiff-necked administration, its implied support of pro-choicers, and its disrespect for the teachings of the Church on abortion. There were about a dozen groups who were as frustrated as we were with the university's full-speed-ahead down the road to secularism. They were ready and willing to help. We met with reps from the campus Right to Life chapter, the Cardinal Newman Society, the Catholic League, and others. One way or another, we wanted to send our message to *everyone* at that game.

A single-page flyer was one prong and we organized an army of more than two hundred (including some grads from the *Act For Aquinas* group) who were ready to do the legwork—handing it out at the stadium gates, putting it under windshield wipers on every parked car within walking distance and at all local motels, distributing it outside campus buildings, and leaving copies at newsstands. Each would be wearing a red armband with a "LIFE" imprint.

It was to the point and pulled no punches. The *Sentinel* had agreed to run it on game day below the fold on page one. We all shared the greatly discounted cost of printing some 40,000 copies:

> WELCOME to the first football contest between two
> citadels of learning founded by the Congregation of

the Holy Cross. We hope that *your_*team—Stonehill College or the University of Notre Dame—comports itself today in the best traditions of the game. Whatever the outcome, it should be an event of joy for us all!

There is another reason to celebrate. Notre Dame's oldest alumnus, Gerard Finn of Chicago, Class of 1934, today is celebrated as the school's only living centenarian. Regrettably, university schedule conflicts have prevented this occasion from being celebrated during half-time ceremonies today, as originally planned.

As you may know, the *South Bend Sentinel* has verified that Mr. Finn came to America as a three-month *in utero* child and passenger on the ill-fated RMS *Titanic*. As such, he is today the only living survivor of that disaster in 1912. (It is no coincidence that Mr. Finn bears the baptismal name Gerard. St. Gerard Majella is the patron saint of motherhood —and unborn children in particular.)

Unfortunately, the president of Notre Dame, Reverend Henry Pankey, and the Board of Fellows have failed to acknowledge, for whatever reason, that fact. In doing so, they have also given silent assent and comfort to those who do not believe that life begins at conception. For the leadership of the world's most famous Catholic academic institution to remain silent, it is a grave denial of the natural law and a source of considerable scandal to Catholics and non-Catholics.

We pray that this institution, dedicated 170 years ago to Our Lady, may soon return to its founding principles and its mission—as a Catholic, not a secular, university.

Also present today is eighty-seven-year old Mary Dolan Jamieson of Unity, MO, the daughter of *Titanic* passenger Edward Dolan. As the *Titanic* sank, Edward Dolan pulled Gerry Finn's mother, with child, into a lifeboat. Now that littlest life on board *Titanic* a century ago is today's guest of honor.

November 3, 2012

The university had been less than enthusiastic to provide the *Sentinel* with the usual two sets of press credentials for the game, but that was fine with us. Jack Graney would join the three-hundred-plus journalists reporting from the sixty-foot high press box on the stadium's west side, while I would be one of four accompanying Gerry Finn on the field in his "Swifty" wheelchair. My old department had arranged for us to enter from section 100, a temporary honorary entrance set up for Gerry's use only, on the north.

We'd be escorted to the tunnel and park briefly under the goal posts long enough for some photographs and an introduction of Gerry. Some of our friends from Sports Info had probably put their jobs on the line to do this, but they were believers. Jessica from the alumni office, Gerry's son Don, and one of the young aide-de-camp's would be with me. The four of us would settle Gerry just to the right of the ND bench, close to the twenty-yard line.

By the start of Halloween week, Massachusetts plates were everywhere and strangers were talking about the fifty "yahd" line and "Fahther" so-and-so. A sea of black capes, cassocks, and birettas was washing across campus. The ND-Stonehill game had clearly magnetized what appeared to be the entire congregational roster of Holy Cross priests. It was their one chance to say, "I was there."

We were all delighted to greet Father Charlie Donahue after eight months of separation and to welcome "the piper's daughter" Mary Dolan Jamieson to campus. She and her son Michael had complimentary rooms at the new Fairfield Inn.

My friend Ed Wagner had a room in town and we all got together when we could. I was able to take a small group of Ed's student journalists on a quick tour of the *Sentinel* one morning. I had eight of Ed's friends staying at my place including a crusty old Yankee named Lou Gasparini, Stonehill's oldest alum. He and Mike Meaney spent most of one night in Leahy's lying to each other.

Shelby had four ladies and Paul was hosting Father Donahue and eight other Stonehill faculty members. The week passed in a blur and then suddenly it was Thursday, All Saints Day, and Gerry Finn was back among us, wearing sunglasses, a Cubs cap, and a jacket that looked like a buffalo skin.

He pinched the collar. "Pure leather. I've had this since 1940. Good as new. Now tell me I don't have to make a speech. I've used up all the jokes I know and I just want to watch the game."

"God bless you, Gerry. No speeches. Just wallow in the adulation and toss a few waves to everyone. We'll be going in from the north end about forty-five minutes before kickoff and stop under the goal posts long enough for you to be introduced and get pictures of you and Mary Jamieson together. Then we'll go past the crowd on the ND side and settle in on the field just past the bench. About the twenty-yard line. All you have to do is wave when you're announced and maybe a few more times while we walk behind the bench."

Friday was All Souls Day. Jessica called me at work to say that she'd been scolded by one of Father Pankey's lieutenants for not setting up a meeting with Gerry and the university president. She was one of us and I could talk to her. "He's a hypocrite," I said. "And he ain't seen nuttin yet."

I remembered the birthday cake. It was to be a work of art: a 2' x 2' replica of the ND stadium with a candle marking each of the one hundred yards.

"Has the cake been delivered yet?"

"It's in the fridge at Sorin's. Seats reserved for one hundred. A welcoming banner in front. It will be a blast."

"Did you-know-who ... ever respond to your invite?"

"Not a word. But I can't imagine he wouldn't show. A good chance for him to mend some fences."

I didn't see that happening. The Reverend Pankey would probably assume the cake was for him.

A Colorado "raining-fire-in-the-sky" sunset that night heralded ideal football weather for Saturday. About half of our "LIFE" organization met before dawn, donned their red armbands, and headed out to begin distributing our one-pager. A second wave would do the same just before noon.

So it was Judgment Day for the Northeast-10 champion Skyhawks and the faltering 2-6 Irish. Kickoff was at 2:00 PM, the last daylight savings time day of the year. Tomorrow, we'd drop the clocks back an hour. Our plans to give Gerry a fitting celebration were on track. I should have been in high spirits, but I wasn't. I felt like a cat in a room full of rocking chairs.

We met at noon Saturday and Jessica gave us all our laminated, chained blue stadium passes with "FIELD" printed in gold. She hung them around our necks like Olympic medals. Then we accompanied Gerry to the Grotto in his Swifty, stopping every few feet, it seemed, for him to receive handshakes or hugs. Everyone seemed to know him. Our one-pager (some of which now littered benches, sidewalks, and statues) was obviously being read. When we arrived, Gerry moved himself up to the kneeling rail and we all followed. I knelt and prayed first for him and second for some peace and reconciliation to come to this university. There was a large crowd there and when we knelt, almost all of them did, wherever they were standing. No one stood until Gerry left the railing. It was a sight I would never forget.

From there we moved to Bond Hall where the ND band was just beginning its traditional pregame concert on the steps. We had made arrangements and I didn't want us to miss this one. The crowd parted like the Red Sea to make room up front for Gerry. The band didn't miss a beat and segued snappily into "Happy Birthday." It had to be a first in ND home game band concert history and everyone joined in singing.

It was close to 1 PM when we arrived at the stadium north end and were ushered inside like visiting dignitaries.

"I sure wish my roommates could have seen this," said Gerry. "They used to say accountants all lead dull lives. They called me Bob Cratchit. They were always trying to fix me up with Lulu Belle, the queen of the Palais Royale."

It was exactly 1:15 PM when we came out of the tunnel and parked Gerry and his Swifty under the goalposts. Mary Jamieson was waiting and a guy from my old Sports Info group was there with his camera. I had it synchronized with my pal Brian Hargrove from the *Chicago Tribune*. The Public Address system snapped on immediately and a commanding voice boomed out:

Ladies and Gentlemen,

Please let us direct your attention to the north end of the stadium where, under the goal posts, you will see Notre Dame's oldest alumnus, Gerry Finn, class of 1934.

Today is Gerry's one hundredth birthday. So please join me in wishing him a most happy birthday.

Thank you all very much.

I might mention, in case anyone here doesn't know, Gerry is also the last living survivor of the *Titanic* disaster on April 14, 1912. He was on that ship and there is no disputing it. Our Blessed Mother atop the Dome kept him alive for just this day.

I'd also like to mention that exactly one hundred years ago today, Notre Dame's football team opened its 1912 season with a three to nothing win over Pittsburgh. They were undefeated in seven games that year and scored 390 points against twenty-seven for the opposition.

So welcome to you all today, thank you, and once again, happy one hundred to Gerry! We love you!

It was another highly emotional moment. Mary was still standing next to Gerry with her arm around his neck.

"I was there, you know, Mary," I heard him say. "With your dad."

"My dad and the good Lord both held you in their hands," she replied.

I could hardly contain myself as we accompanied Gerry past the waving crowd and to our places just beyond the Irish bench. I hoped, as much as I had ever hoped anything, that the Reverend Henry Pankey was already in his seat and had witnessed the whole event and heard every word. I scanned the preferred seating section behind me to see if there was a cloud of black smoke rising anywhere. He would also surely have read a copy of our handout by now and would no doubt be fuming.

We settled in and Gerry had his binoculars trained on the Stonehill team working out down at our end of the field.

"Not a whole lot of beef out there, Josh," he said. "Didn't they feed you guys up there in Massachusetts?"

"If you're talking about the government, Gerry, what they feed us mostly is a lot of baloney. That's how it was when I lived there and I don't think it's changed any."

He slapped the sides of his Swifty. "Did you know that Rockne coached his team from a wheelchair back in 1929? It's true. Had a bum leg for a while."

My heart was with Stonehill, but a look at the two teams running through their warm-ups out there and it was obvious that a Division II team like the Skyhawks didn't stand a Chinaman's chance against a Division I home team that had just been up against Michigan, Michigan State, Miami, Oklahoma, and others. It was called ND's "Apocalyptic Schedule" and this was the only breather on it.

When it came time for the coin flip, I know that Jessica and others were thinking of earlier plans for Gerry to do the honors, later squelched by the administration. What was it we had called Father Pankey months ago? *"Rather mean-spirited."* Yes, too true.

The Irish won the toss and elected to receive. The whistle blew and then the ball was in the air, twitching and trembling its way downfield. A mediocre kick and the worst fears of Skyhawk coach Rob Leake were quickly realized. The receiver scooped it up, followed a pair of blockers down the middle and sped into the end zone almost untouched. Notre Dame 7, Stonehill 0.

By the middle of the second quarter, the Irish were up 24-0 and Coach Sean Noonan pulled most of his starters. Wide receiver Shaquel Walker had already added two TD receptions to his portfolio, as well as fifteen negative yards to his team's stats for taunting.

With only thirty seconds left until halftime, Stonehill's stocky Tyler Smith broke free and danced sixty-five yards to pay dirt. Irish 24, Skyhawks 7.

While the band performed, we waited for someone to arrive and award Gerry his centenarian certificate. And waited. And waited. Before the Reverend Pankey had finished his "Eight for Excellence" eye-glazing spiel, both teams were back on the field. Whatever comments Stonehill's Father Maloney had intended to say went forever unsaid.

Meanwhile, Jessica was speechless with anger. She'd spent ten minutes on her cell phone with no results except to be told that the presentation to Gerry would be made later that day. It didn't take a wizard to guess that someone in the Main Building was unhappy with Gerry's pregame introduction and was retaliating. Shelby had called me on my cell to say that many of our team were being arrested and detained by campus police. Their red LIFE armbands were being confiscated.

Our spirits were lifted by the arrival of a large white and bluish bird, a seagull of some sort, that landed between the end zone and us. It appeared to be in no hurry to leave and stalked around, ignoring the arm waving of an usher. No doubt some of the writers high above us were already identifying it as a Skyhawk come to mourn.

Whatever hopes Stonehill might have had to regroup were dashed early in the third quarter. With ND's starters back on the field, things looked glum for the Skyhawks.There seemed to be no way they could defend against Irish quarterback Luke Reese's clothes-liners to Shaquel Walker who sashayed, one hand holding the ball ahead of him, into the end zone for his third TD.

By the time the band had struck up its traditional *1812 Overture* to start the final quarter, the score was 38–7 and the Las Vegas thirty-point spread appeared to be safe. But when the Skyhawks responded with a field goal five minutes later, it was 38–10 and the bookies were no doubt squirming.

Meanwhile our visiting bird had strutted almost beneath our feet, looked us over and decided to stay. With a flutter of his white wings, he (she?) landed lightly on Gerry's headrest and settled in.

"Keep an eye on him, guys," said Gerry. "I don't want this leather jacket decorated."

High up in the press box, Shelby, who had been employed as a gofer, peered down at the scene below.

"Herring Gull," she said.

Tim Fox, elderly sports editor from the *Indianapolis Star,* glanced over. "What? What did she say? Harangody? Good Lord, woman."

Gerry had been sitting quietly but now he raised his arm and waved it slowly at someone on the other side of the field.

"Who's that, Gerry?" I asked.

"I don't know her name," he replied. "Never did. But she's someone I met at the Grotto my freshman year."

I must have misheard him. I'll ask him later.

ND's coach Noonan kept his starters in despite grumbling from the Stonehill bench and a smattering of boos from the crowd. With just under two minutes left, Irish QB Luke Reese rolled to his right, tracking Walker who was coming down the sideline in our direction. He let it fly.

It all happened so quickly that none of us had time to react. The ball was perfectly thrown and Walker had only to reach up and pull it in. But the seagull had launched itself from Gerry's headrest at just the wrong moment. The football grazed the bird and sent it tumbling to the field. The ball bounced crazily on the sideline and Walker's momentum carried him full bore into the side of Gerry's Swifty. Both hit the ground heavily. Walker was padded. Gerry was not.

There was no miracle to witness. No divine, celestial hand reaching down to intervene. Gerry's head was twisted to one side and hung down at a contorted angle.

We were all blind with tears by the time the medics had taken him away on the injured-players cart. The crowd, yet to realize that Gerry's life had come to a sudden end on his field of dreams, stood and applauded. But there was no return wave from the body on the cart.

In the preferred seating section, Stonehill president Father Jake Maloney jumped over the railing and followed the cart on the run. The Reverend Pankey remained seated, his eyes on the field.

Irish wide receiver Shaquel Walker had risen and walked away from the accident without a second glance back. It was only later when we viewed the replay that we saw him kick the injured herring gull as he passed it.

Notre Dame won the game 38–10. But they lost so much more.

On Tuesday, November 6, funeral services for Gerard Finn were held at Holy Name Cathedral on Chicago's North Side. More than two hundred were in attendance and some fifty of them, friends and relatives, discovered parking tickets decorating their cars when they exited the church. Another half dozen found that their cars had been towed.

On the same day, voters across the nation went to the polls and reelected Mubaraq El Baba to another four-year term. The administration rejected suggestions that the blanket government amnesty granted by

Executive Order to thirteen million illegal aliens (and giving them voting rights) was a factor.

It would be a long time before Shelby and I could even begin to comprehend it all. There was something in Notre Dame Stadium that day that never left us. Gerry and Mary beneath the goal posts. The wave from Gerry to an unseen woman who would have had to be over ninety-years-old. And that bird. That bird. It was hard not to remember that childhood hymn to Mary:
Gentle mother, peaceful dove,
teach us wisdom; teach us love.

We would never know.

Peter K. Connolly

Note

Translated from the Arabic in the Islamic Year 1608 AH* (Year 2179 Gregorian Calendar)

The manuscript for the preceding work of fiction was one of several recovered during the years following the 1512 AH (Year 2088 Greg.) subterranean seismological 'incident' in the territory of what was known as northern Indiana and which resulted in the deaths of hundreds of thousands of people. The epicenter of the upheaval was determined to be an underground cave of boulders.*

The setting for the story was a military training camp and indoctrination center for infidels known as "Notre Dame of Lakes." The icon for this center was a gold-plated dome with a sculpted woman atop. It was probably located somewhere just north of the present Center for Quaran Studies of the Holy Prophet and the Pavilion of the Islamic Warrior adjoining the twenty-five-story Masjid Yeni Dünya (New World Mosque).

The lakes after which the earlier training camp took its name do not exist and some question if they ever did. The imaginative events described herein would have occurred sometime around 1433 AH (Year 2012 Greg.), approximately fifty years before the founding of the New Islamic Republic in the former Organized American States.*

* In the year of the *Hijra*.